The Funky Chicken

A Christmas Novella

Melinda Eye-Cooper

For David

Copyright © 2013 by Melinda Eye-Cooper

Every autumn Dad drove down old logging trails in search of trees to cut into firewood. Sometimes I ventured along but never did much work. Dad buzzed through wood with a chainsaw and my two older brothers loaded it into the back of the pickup truck. The loud chainsaw scared me so I stayed as far away from Dad as I could when he used it. When he finished and turned off the chainsaw, he placed it in the bed of the truck then we kids climbed into the cab for the drive back home. The heater in the truck warmed us as we sat close together in the front seat and a wonderful feeling of happiness came over me as I sat squished between Dad and my older brother. Their pants were covered with saw dust and I inhaled the fresh smell of oak shavings and smiled. I pretended I loved autumn and that it was my favorite time of year. I did love it when the leaves changed colors but it wasn't really my favorite season.

When we got back to the house, the boys unloaded the wood and stacked the pieces neatly into a rank near the backdoor. Dad put the chainsaw in the shed and they all went inside the house. I stayed outside and stared at the fresh rank of wood we'd burn in our stove the coming winter. It was the same thing at every house that I knew of in Shirley, Missouri in 1977. Every family used a wood stove to keep their houses warm in the winter time just like we did. They either cut firewood or else they bought it from someone else who cut wood for extra money. I couldn't help but wonder if going out into the woods to chop firewood felt anything like going into the woods to chop down a Christmas tree. I figured I'd probably never know.

I inhaled the crisp autumn air and closed my eyes as a smile spread across my lips because winter was just around the corner.

Chapter One

The Class Tree

"Please let Anna put the icicles on the tree," Mrs. Wise instructed. She dug through a cardboard box on the floor full of Christmas decorations for our class tree and pulled out a beautiful paper angel covered in glitter that some former student made and held it up.

"Perfect." She showed it off to the class. Everyone admired the carefully carved paper angel and a round of applause broke out for the perfect Christmas tree topper.

"Now Anna, when you finish putting the icicles on the tree then you can clip the angel on the top of the tree!" She smiled at me with kind, dark eyes hidden behind glasses. Her black hair glistened with streaks of silver and dangled loosely from the bun that twisted around the back of her head.

I beamed with delight. Mrs. Wise let me decorate almost the entire Christmas tree all by myself. She taught my class at Shirley School where I was in the third grade. There were only four classes at my school - first grade, second grade, third grade and fourth grade. My class only had nine children in it which I enjoyed because we got a lot of attention. Somehow Mrs. Wise knew that at my house we didn't have a Christmas tree. I don't know how she knew it but she did. So, she did the nicest thing and let our class tree be *my* Christmas tree.

I flung the soft, slippery silver strings by the handful onto the tree -- a few here and a few there. When I ran out of them, I went back over the tree and pulled apart any clumps of icicles that I found and spread them out evenly. I took a few steps back to examine my work. Mrs. Wise examined my work, too.

"You've done a wonderful job, Anna." She praised and then turned to the class, "Hasn't she done a great job, class?" She smiled and the class cheered in agreement as she handed me the paper angel for the top of the tree. I held the beautiful angel in my hand and pinched the clothespin glued to the back of the angel to snap it onto a branch of the tree. I stood on a chair but still couldn't reach the top. Mrs. Wise gave me a boost and I clipped the angel to the top of the tree as best I could. Then she helped me down and I wiped the glitter from my hands onto my jeans. I took my seat with the other children as she plugged in the lights.

The class chorused a medley of "Ooh's and Ah's" and I joined in with them. It had to be the *most spectacular* tree I'd ever seen in my entire life! There were cut out snowflakes and paper chains made out of red and green construction paper hanging all over it. A strand of popcorn wrapped around the tree five times. Each of us fashioned a decoration made out of Styrofoam and straight pins and colored sequins. They now dangled from the limbs and reflected the lights from the tree and mesmerized me. I couldn't believe that I helped make something as beautiful as our third grade class Christmas tree.

The bell rang and I slowly got up to leave along with my classmates. Everyone ran out the door as fast as they could without getting into trouble for running but I didn't want to go a minute before I had to so that I could keep admiring the Christmas tree. I stood and stared for as long as I dared without missing the bus.

"Thank you for your help today with the tree." Mrs. Wise patted me on the back as I left her classroom.

"You're welcome." I gleamed with pride and went outside with the rest of the class to catch the bus.

I left school with a feeling that I couldn't quite explain. The boogers were freezing inside my nose but somehow I felt all warm and fuzzy inside. I kept the image of the tree in my head all night. It seemed to be stamped into my brain. I even used it to put myself to sleep. Over and over I thought about putting on every single decoration until I drifted off. My dreams were filled with sparkling sequined balls and glittery paper angels.

"Rise and shine! Rivulet! Hit the deck! Roll 'em out! Out of bed, sleepy heads!" Mom came through the house yelling as she passed each bedroom doorway wearing the peach nightgown and robe we got her for Christmas the year before. That's how she got us kids out of bed each morning. Her short, dark hair kinked into curls around her face. My little sister, Ruthie, was the spitting image of Mom except her hair was blond. Their eyes and eyelashes were both dark. I guess I looked like my Dad.

I crawled out of bed while Ruthie still lay there snoozing with her thumb stuck in her mouth. *Kindergarteners,* I thought and then yelled at her, "Get up! Mom said!" She rolled over and pulled the blanket over her head.

"Shut up. I don't have to get up yet!" She whined from underneath the covers.

"Uh-huh!" I said and jerked the blanket off of her. Her twisted up nightgown clung to her waist revealing bare legs covered in goose bumps. She wore her favorite pair of red socks - the ones that she continued to wear almost every day (without getting them washed) until they were stinky and stiff. She feared they'd get lost in the laundry room if she took them off and she'd never see them again. Laundry stayed stacked knee deep in our laundry room and Mom washed clothes every day. She couldn't get it caught up with eight people living in the house.

"I'm cold! Give that back!" Ruthie grabbed the blanket.

"Get in trouble then. I don't care!" I snapped. I hoped she did get in trouble. She deserved it. She always got away with things that I couldn't get away with. Plus, she sucked her thumb until the skin on it shriveled up and a knot formed on the knuckle. Our parents tried again and again to get her to stop. They got the idea from someone to put toothache medicine on her thumb to keep her from sucking it. So, one night they decided to give it a try. They put the medicine on her shriveled up thumb to see if it would work.

"You're trying *poison* me! You're trying to *kill* me!" she whined. "Everybody in this house *hates* me!"

"Nobody hates you, Ruthie. You're not going to die from toothache medicine." Mom told her, "but if you don't stop sucking your thumb you're going to *stunt* its growth and then you'll have one regular thumb and one short stubby one!"

Ruthie stomped to the bathroom and washed her thumb in the sink. She stuck it back inside of her mouth and marched into the living room where everyone sat watching television. Once she had everyone's attention, she wiped a tear from her cheek and said to no one in particular, "I'm *not* going to stop sucking my thumb. It's my thumb and

I'll suck it if I want to!" She plopped down on the end of the couch and glared at the television. Mom and Dad gave up on that idea and went to watching television, too.

After that failure, they decided to try bribery. They offered her a new tricycle if she would stop sucking her thumb. Of course, she gladly agreed to stop but as soon as she got the new red tricycle with the little silver bell on the handlebars, she rode it all around the carport with her thumb stuck in her mouth. The only time she took it out was to ring the little silver bell. All of us glared at her and she didn't say a word because she didn't have to. She won. The look on her face told the tale. "*Ha-ha. I got a new bike and I'm still sucking my thumb!*"

Sometimes I wanted to clobber her. Sometimes I loved her. She'd learned the art of manipulation early in life and I couldn't seem to get the hang of it. She was cute with her big brown eyes with long eyelashes and blond hair. I felt plain with my dishwater blond hair and green eyes.

"Get in here and get some breakfast!" Mom yelled again as she sat at the kitchen table with an electric skillet flipping pancakes. I sat down at the table and waited for my favorite breakfast to be served. When I finally got the steaming hot stack of fluffy pancakes I slathered them in butter and maple syrup. They were *heavenly*. My two older brothers gobbled theirs down and were already waiting for seconds by the time I finished my first pancake. They ate like porkers but Mom always said, "They're growing boys!" I guess it was true. They were growing fast but I didn't understand why they ate so fast. It seemed like they were afraid that somebody else might get more than them or they might not get seconds or *thirds*.

My older sister sat at the table and nibbled on a pancake. She reminded me of a glamour queen with her long brown hair and green eyes. She attended high school in town. My oldest sister, Kate, was very pregnant with my first niece or nephew. My parents didn't seem to like her husband much. Mom never called him by his real name, Richard, but referred to him by his secret nickname - *Weasel*.

My favorite older sister, Elizabeth, recently exchanged vows and moved away too. I tried to hide my unhappy feelings about the whole thing. Not only did my favorite sister leave but she took my favorite thing with her when she went. The piano! I'd been taking lessons and adored it. But when she moved out, the piano went with her. Luckily, she only lived a mile away so I could go to her house sometimes and play it still. It just wasn't the same though.

My little brother looked like me with blond hair and green eyes. The front teeth in his little mouth were rotten because he fell on the coffee table and hit his teeth. He'd lost his balance learning how to walk and the dentist said they were bruised and nothing could be done. His smile wouldn't show white front teeth again until he grew in some new ones when he turned six or so. I don't think he cared much about it though.

After I ate my pancakes, I got dressed and ready to catch the bus. We kids waited at the bus stop at the end of our driveway with some of the neighbors until the bus picked us up. At the next stop, my friend, Nella, got on the bus and plopped down in the seat across from me. She didn't say a word. I couldn't tell whether she got mad about something at home or just woke up on the wrong side of the bed. Nella opened up a paperback book and busied herself reading. It was one of her talents. She could read a book faster than anybody else that I knew. Nella would also share her wardrobe from time to time. There were only two kids in her family so she usually had nice things. Sometimes she would let me borrow something to wear if a special occasion came up and I saw something in her closet that I liked. Even though she towered me by a couple of inches, her clothes still fit me pretty good. Most of my clothes were hand-me-downs from my cousins.

"Good morning," I offered.

She looked up from her book long enough to smile and murmur, "Good morning." Then she engrossed herself again in her story flipping pages like lightning.

There were two brothers who got on the bus at Nella's bus stop. The first one, Mike, stood tall and was thin with dark hair and dark eyes. He loved to go to church and would wait for the church bus to come pick him up to take him to the Missionary Baptist Church on Grassy Hollow Road on Wednesday nights. His younger brother, Buster, was short, stout and blond headed. He always made trouble and wouldn't step inside of the church house unless forced to on Easter or Christmas. If he didn't start a fight with somebody on the bus then he passed horrid gas that made everybody put down their windows even on the coldest winter day. He just liked to be that way. The boys sat down in seats across from each other near the back of the bus.

The bus jerked us around when it went around curves or hit chugholes in the pavement. Our bus driver kept a club by the front seat although I never actually saw her use it on anyone. One time, I thought I might get a chance to see her swing it at someone. A fight broke out between the two brothers after they got on the bus one morning at Nella's stop and the bus driver whipped out the club just as Mike pushed Buster up the row of seats toward the front of the bus. They punched each other and fell over into one of the empty seats wrestling. The bus driver raised her voice above the fighting brothers and threatened Buster with the club. He shook his fist at his taller brother and swore they weren't finished. Everyone watched as Buster, red with anger, left the bus and strutted up his driveway glaring back at his brother with a fury boiling inside. Mike sat back down in his seat and wiped a few drops of blood from his nose. My glamour queen sister handed him a tissue and he nodded his gratitude as he wiped his upper lip and nostrils. The bus driver put the club back in its place and drove the bus on down the road toward Shirley School for her first drop off just like nothing even happened. That's as close as I got to witnessing the use of the club on someone. I never did know what they were fighting about but I knew I didn't want to be around if they started fighting again. Buster meant business.

When I got to school I couldn't wait to see the classroom Christmas tree. The bus pulled in front of the school and the bus driver pulled the lever that opened the door. I scrambled out and saw two fourth graders already raising the flag up the flag pole. I ran around to the side of the school where the doors to the gymnasium were and pulled one open. There were several people hanging around talking but I got to my classroom as fast as I could.

Then I saw it. Our beautiful Christmas tree glowed in all of its glorious beauty! The lights were already plugged in and the tree sparkled in the dark classroom. I gave the tree a good look and felt of its branches. Mrs. Wise sat at her desk in front of the classroom and observed me over the top rim of her glasses. She smiled as I placed my face in the limbs of the tree as far as I could until the prickly branches began to poke me. I inhaled the wonderful, rich cedar fragrance.

Then I moseyed around to the other classrooms to see what their trees looked like. A large cedar tree stood in the corner of each classroom decorated with hand-made decorations. Usually, the fourth graders won for the best tree. Maybe because they were older, I don't know, but this year I believed there was no beating our tree - probably because of all my personal touches to the tree. I practically decorated it myself!

I met up with my best friend, Anna Lee. She'd blossomed early and already wore a bra. I didn't figure I'd need a bra for many years to come.

"Here, I brought you something." Anna Lee handed me a brown paper bag. I peeked inside.

"Good night nurse!" I gushed and ran to the girls' bathroom where I pulled a *bra* out of the bag!

"I outgrew this one. You can have it!" Anna Lee smiled. Her thoughtfulness touched me. I examined the bra. There were no cups like I imagined there would be but the material across the front stretched and felt soft. I went into a stall and put it on. *It fit!* Of course, I didn't need it but it was still fun to wear like maybe I might need it soon. The bra felt tight and a little scratchy around the back where the clasps were but when I put my shirt on over it I felt like a *grown up*. Anna Lee smiled at me as we went into class and took our seats.

The bell rang and everyone waited in silence for Mrs. Wise to begin class.

"Daniel, please open the shades for us," she instructed.

Daniel stood up and found the cord for the blinds, and slowly pulled on it until sunlight came pouring into the classroom.

"Thank you, Daniel." Mrs. Wise said, "Class, please take out your reading books."

Daniel sat back down in his seat and lifted the top of his desk. He pulled out his reading book and placed it on his desk and flipped through the pages until he found the story we would be reading. Somehow, the glasses he wore slid all the way down to the end of his nose and so he pushed them back up where they belonged with his pointer finger. Daniel seemed older than the rest of us for some reason and sometimes needed extra help with his work. Mrs. Wise always stopped and patiently helped him. I felt kind of sorry for him for no reason in particular. He stayed to himself a lot and didn't say much.

There were two sisters in class who lived right next to the school and could walk every day. Fitz could run faster than anybody else in Shirley School, even faster than the Fourth graders! Bridget was in my class, too. She always brought cookies from the grocery store with icing on them that Mom would never buy because they were too expensive. Sometimes Bridget would share or swap something for a bite. Jill sat next to Daniel. Her long, dark hair curled everywhere and her eyes smiled anytime her mouth did. The cutest boy I ever saw sat behind me. He had blond hair and long dark eyelashes with big brown eyes like my stinker little sister. It looked pretty good on a boy.

Jill began to read as we all followed along in our reading books. She stumbled over a few words but got through it pretty well, I thought. When Mrs. Wise called on me to read, I read in my best voice. I tried hard to pronounce the words right and to make the sentences flow in a nice rhythm. But I got stuck on a word I'd never seen before. I stopped reading and slowly sounded it out. "Chic….uh…go," I read and then said it faster in my sentence. "Chicago." Only I pronounced it with the "uh" sound in the middle and everyone busted out laughing. A grin spread across my face as I realized it was the city, Chicago - the one in Illinois.

Chapter Two

A Secret Tree

"Christmas is almost here!" A kid announced on the back of the bus as I rode home from school that day.

"I can't wait!" another kid said and then the two of them took to talking about their Christmas lists and what they hoped Santa would bring them. I never bothered making a Christmas list. There didn't seem to be much point.

There was only one more week till Christmas. I chewed on my bottom lip and wiped the steam from the school bus window so that I could admire the decorations on the way home from school. No matter where I looked, there were signs here or there that families were getting ready to celebrate the wonderful holiday. Christmas trees glowed in picture windows. Beautiful wreaths dangled on the front doors of many of the homes in Shirley.

As we made the stop to drop off my classmate, Daniel and his brother and sister, they rushed inside their house. A lovely tree stood right in front of their living room window. Dazzling lights hung around the gutters of their house. A plastic Santa face lit up their front door and even the trees in their yard were lit up by strands of lights.

I turned my face toward the front of the bus as jealousy crept over me. I wished that I could have lights draped around the trees in my front yard! Why couldn't I have them draped around window frames and gutters and doorways? It just looked so fun. But when the bus dropped me off at my house along with my siblings there were no lights. No wreath hung on our front door. There were no decorations or even a sign that Christmas was just around the corner. Still, the plain brown brick house with the white carport across the front, beckoned me home.

As I walked toward the front door something caught my eye. A lovely little pine tree grew in the woods across the fence. Though somewhat hidden behind a bigger pine tree, I could see that it seemed to be the perfect size for a Christmas tree. Then a wonderful, happy thought crossed my mind. I figured since I couldn't have a tree inside the house then I would have my own Christmas tree in the woods! It would be my own secret Christmas tree and nobody would know about it except for me.

The only problem was the little pine tree wasn't on our property. It sprouted on old man Gibson's land. The tall man often wandered his property looking for wild mushrooms or carrying a bucket to pick blackberries with. Sometimes, he carried a shotgun in the crook of one arm in case he happened upon a rabbit or squirrel. I wondered what he'd think if he found a decorated Christmas tree on his property? Would he be glad or would he be mad? Cause sometimes he'd act real nice and friendly if he saw you in the store with Mom. Then other times, if he caught you on his land looking for arrowheads or swinging on monkey vines, then he'd run you off and tell you to stay off of his property. My older brothers said that one time he pulled the shotgun on them. But I really didn't know if they were telling me the truth or not. Still, I just didn't know what old man Gibson would do if he caught me on his property decorating a pine tree.

After a bit of consideration, I decided I'd take the risk. I ran inside the house and dropped my books on the bed. I racked my brain trying to figure out what on earth I could use to decorate a little pine tree with because there were no Christmas decorations in our house that I knew of. I wandered around the house looking for something, opening closets and cabinets until I ended up in the kitchen. The only place I could think of that might have something worth finding was the junk drawer. Surely I could find something useful in that wonderful drawer full of everything.

"Whatcha doin'?" Ruthie asked with her thumb stuck in the corner of her mouth. She stood beside me in the kitchen watching every move I made.

"None ya," I said and rummaged through the junk drawer looking for hooks or pins or something.

"Guess what?" She didn't wait for me to guess. "I got to go out to eat after school today," she bragged. Her big brown eyes gleamed and she tilted her head with pride.

"Big *hairy* deal." I ignored her pestilence and kept digging. With all the stuff inside that drawer I couldn't find one useful thing for decorating a little pine tree. I stopped digging and stood with my hands on my hips and thought hard. Finally, an idea hit me.

"Where's the tin foil?" I asked.

"Down here." Ruthie opened up the cabinet beside the stove.

I opened the box of foil and pulled out a couple of feet of it and tore it off. I put the box back in the cabinet as she stared at me with a curious sort of look on her round face.

"What are you gonna do with that?" she inquired.

"None of your bees wax," I said as I snuck it into my room. She followed right behind me.

"Get out!" I raised my voice but only slightly because I didn't want anyone else to know what I had my heart set on.

"No!" She stomped her foot.

"Just let me have some peace!" I pleaded but she flung herself down beside me on the bed.

"It's my room, too!" She reminded me and laid there watching my every move. I rolled my eyes at her and gave up.

"Fine. Stay then." I said and realized that she'd won again. It wasn't important right then so I picked up the foil and carefully started to tear it into thin strips.

"What are you gonna do with that?" She asked again unable to contain her curiosity.

I sighed.

"If you must know Ruthie, I'm using these for decorations." I secretly hoped she wouldn't care and she'd leave me alone but instead I roused her desire to create something fun.

Her eyes lit up. Those big, brown, sparkly eyes with long eyelashes were looking up at me full of excitement and *hope*.

"Can I help?" She begged. "*Please* Anna! I wanna make decorations!"

I thought about it for a second. Even I couldn't resist those brown eyes.

"Sure." I gave in, "Just don't tell anybody. It's a secret."

"I won't," she said and promised to stick a needle in her eye if she told anyone.

That serious promise told me she'd do her best to keep our secret. So, together we tore the tin foil into strips and made circles out of them by twisting the ends. We scrunched them in different places and tried our best to make them look like something bought or at least something nice enough to decorate a Christmas tree with. Finally, we carried them out the back door of the house where no one could see us and took them over to the little pine tree on our neighbors' property. We piled the foil rings on the ground and began to put them on the tree. All the while we listened carefully for footsteps or dogs in the woods behind us in case old man Gibson snuck up on us with a shotgun. Once, I hushed Ruthie by placing my finger on my lips and we listened as carefully as we could. Something scurried behind us. When we looked closely, we could see a couple of little grey rabbits playing in the brush not far from us. We released a sigh of relief and finished our task of decorating the tree with tin foil. Slowly, the little pine tree started to look a little like a Christmas tree.

When we finished we were very proud of ourselves. Ruthie clapped her hands together and smiled. I looked at the pitiful pine tree. It didn't compare to the classroom tree. There was really no way that it could be. We didn't have any real decorations. I thought about the snowflakes, chains and popcorn strings we created in class. *Maybe we could make some of those?*

"Let's go see what else we can find to fix the tree up with," I said and we climbed the fence and went back inside the house. We shed our coats and started scrounging around the kitchen. We couldn't find any construction paper or any popcorn but we did have notebook paper. So, we started making snowflakes out of it. I folded the notebook paper in half several times and then began to cut pieces out. After several failed attempts, I put the scissors down.

"These don't look so good." I frowned and held up the chopped up pieces of paper that didn't resemble snowflakes at all. "I can't remember exactly how we had made them in class," I said as Ruthie picked up the little bitty pieces of paper everywhere.

Ruthie thought as she cleaned and finally suggested, "What about crepe paper?"

"Yeah! That would work!" I agreed. I couldn't believe she came up with such a good idea. Mom kept a box under her bed with ribbons and bows in it for decorating birthday presents or other gifts. Sometimes she'd keep left over wrapping paper and extra party supplies, too. We snuck in her room and pulled it out. Our hopes were soon dashed as we dug through the box. All that we could find were some old red and green bows from who knows when. We tore the bows apart and decided to use them as ribbon. Then my little sister came up with another pretty good idea.

"How about toilet paper?" She suggested with an ornery grin.

"*Toilet paper*?" I scrunched up my nose at the idea. Then after some consideration, I figured it would look pretty good! "Okay!" I said and we grabbed a roll from the bathroom. There were little pink flowers printed on it but I didn't figure it would make any difference from a distance. We hurriedly slipped out the sliding backdoor again with our supplies hidden beneath our coats. We crossed the fence and finished decorating the tree with toilet paper and ribbon. Our work impressed us when we finally stepped back to see how it looked from a distance. The little pine tree came to life with the tin foil circles dangling from its branches along with red and green ribbon wrapped around it. The pink flowered toilet paper draped it from top to bottom and it didn't look half bad!

We looked around one more time before we went home to be sure the property owner hadn't spied us on his land. We didn't see him anywhere so we climbed the fence and went inside to eat supper. Mom was well known throughout the neighborhood for her cooking abilities. If kids were at our house playing and it got to be dinner time, they grabbed a plate with the rest of us and sat down to eat. She'd fixed a pot of her famous vegetable beef soup. It stewed on the stove for hours. When dinner time came, we sat down at the table with our family for a bowl. Ruthie sat next to me and clung to me like never before. I guess I kinda liked it.

That night as we lay down to sleep I felt a little closer to my stinker sister. She hadn't told anybody yet about the tree and I thought she'd keep it our secret. We talked about wrapping up some presents and putting them under the tree for fun. I couldn't believe that across the fence in the woods stood a Christmas tree of our very own.

I tried to sleep but sleep didn't come easy when you slept in the same bed with a thumb sucker. Ruthie was sleeping and sucking. Sleeping and sucking.

Smack, smack, smack! Smack, smack, smack!

It drove me crazy. I tried to make noises to cover up the smacking sound by tapping my hand on the bed rail but I could still hear her.

Smack, smack, smack.

I covered my ears and hummed a tune inside my head. When I

started to drift off, my hand came off my ear and I could hear her again.

Smack. Snore. *Smack.* Snore.

I covered my ears again and hummed Amazing Grace to block her out.

Amazing grace, how sweet the sound...that saved a wretch like me...I once was lost but now I'm found...was blind but now I see....

Finally, her thumb fell out of her mouth and she snoozed. Then I rolled over and went to sleep.

The next morning I woke up cold and shivering. I felt of the bed and it was all wet! The wet spot seemed to be more on my side of the bed! *I didn't wet the bed!* I thought as I sat up and moved my hand across around the cold, wet mattress. Then I flipped on the bedroom light. I looked over at Ruthie. Her wet nightgown was twisted around her waist and revealed soggy underwear. She'd rolled over and peed on me then rolled back over to the dry side of the bed and went to sleep! I steamed as I headed to the bathroom to take a shower.

The hot water calmed me down before Mom made her way through the house with her usual morning wake-up call. I complained to Mom about Ruthie peeing on me and she couldn't seem to stop the smile that spread across her face. She suppressed her laugh but I could see that she found it funny more than anything else. I didn't see the humor in the situation.

My older brothers were sitting at the table with a box of my favorite cereal and a gallon of milk. I brightened up as I got a bowl from the kitchen cabinet and a spoon. Mom rarely bought brand name cereal unless she found a good coupon for it. So, I sat down at the table and excitedly grabbed the box only to discover it already empty!

Empty? As the reality sank in I began to steam again. "You ate the *whole* box?!" I growled as I stared into the empty box of my favorite cereal.

"Yep." They both smirked and were obviously proud of themselves.

I gave them both the stink eye.

"There's a bag of puffed wheat in the cabinet." My oldest brother smacked his cereal as he spoke then he slurped down the milk in the bottom of his bowl. Every smack grated my nerves as I went to the cabinet and pulled out the dreaded bag of puffed wheat. I poured some into my bowl with milk and doused it with sugar.

My oldest brother picked up his empty bowl and spoon to put it in the sink and grabbed the empty box of my favorite cereal to throw it away.

I stared at both of them as I chewed on the cereal that reminded me of munching on a piece of cardboard. I stuck my tongue out at both of them as they left me there to eat that wretched, tasteless puffed wheat cereal.

Chapter Three
No Gift to Give

My spirits lifted when I got to Shirley School and saw our beautiful Christmas tree. Plus, we were going to practice that day for our school Christmas program. We were singing Christmas carols and having a small production. Three boys were going to be the three wise men and then there would be Joseph, Mary and baby Jesus. Baby Jesus would be played by a doll.

When everyone got released from class to practice in the gym, we lined up and found our places on the risers. Our music teacher's two front teeth were big and hung over her bottom lip. She wore her hair pinned way up high on top of her head and looked like a giant ant with her arms stretched up in the air like antenna as she waved us into tempo.

We sang Christmas songs and the wise men found the baby Jesus under the star in the manger. I loved the beautiful story and I felt good being a part of it. I especially loved the part when I sang my solo, *Away in a Manger*. I beamed with pride as I finished. Mrs. Wise smiled at me as I took my place back on the risers. Christmas seemed within reach as we finished practicing for our Christmas program. I could hardly wait.

Saturday finally came and along with that came my friend, Nella. Most every Saturday, after she finished her chores, she'd come over to my house. Our house was full of kids and since we were the closest in age, we played when we weren't fighting.

"I got you a present," Nella sang as we sat in my bedroom talking. My heart stopped beating for a moment because I hadn't gotten her anything and to tell the truth, it hadn't even crossed my mind.

"What is it?" I asked.

"I'm not telling you!" She rolled her eyes at me and pushed her black hair away from her face and tucked it behind her ears. Gold dolphin earrings sparkled on her earlobes. Behind her pale blue eyes ran a streak of something. I don't think it was meanness exactly but something that I didn't trust and couldn't figure out.

"Where's mine?" She inquired.

"I don't have it yet," I admitted and wondered where I would be able to come up with some money to get her something. I began to imagine how much leg scratching I would have to do to come up with enough money to buy a present. Mom loved to get her legs scratched and it was one of the ways that at my age I could earn some extra money. The change I earned could buy penny candy at Bohannon's country store down the road but it didn't seem like nearly enough for a present.

"We'll exchange them next weekend," she informed me as she lit up inside with excitement. "You should see *our* Christmas tree!" she exclaimed. "Can you come over and look at it?" The smile on her face seared through me. She loved rubbing her big fat Christmas tree in my face every year.

I thought for a moment and then said, "Maybe I'll see it when we exchange presents." Truthfully, I'd already seen her Christmas tree through her living room window but didn't mention it to her.

"Okay. Do you want to play a game?"

"Nah. I don't feel like it." Suddenly Christmas made me sad. No tree, no money to buy gifts, friends who rubbed it all in - it just made me depressed.

"Let's go outside then," she continued.

"Nah. Too tired," I mumbled and hoped she'd go home.

"Come on! Don't be lazy! Let's go for a walk." She pulled me up off the bed by grabbing my forearms. Nella liked to pester me until I gave in and did whatever it was she wanted.

"Fine." I drug my feet and followed her outside into the bitter cold where she began to tell me all about the boy at her school that she liked and how he kissed her one day after school. I didn't believe it.

"Bull crap," I said.

"It's true. You can ask him." She knew that I could never ask him because she didn't go to my school in the country. She went to *town* school.

"Well, who cares?" I said.

"I do. Plus, he does, too. You just don't care because you have never been kissed and probably never will be!" Nella sneered and scrunched up her nose at me.

"I'm going inside," I said and headed back to my house.

"*Fine!* I'm going home." She headed up the road and I didn't care. There were no other kids her age in the neighborhood to play with except me. We'd be playing again next weekend probably.

That night, as I lay in bed listening to my sister smacking her thumb, I blocked her out by singing my solo over and over in my head. I saw myself on a great stage with a microphone in my hand belting it out like nobody's business. I dramatically pointed to the manger scene as I sang so that everyone would know that Jesus lay there and lifted my hands up to the Heavens when I finished and took a big bow. The audience broke out into applause and gave me a standing ovation. I felt like a star! Even if it was just in my imagination!

Then above the smacking and my own singing in my head, I heard something strange. I stopped and listened.

What is that? I wondered.

It sounded like moaning or crying. I made my way out of the bedroom and closer to the sound. I saw Mom in the living room watching television with some of the older kids whose bedtimes were later than mine.

I walked by my parents' bedroom and heard the moaning sound coming from in there. I quietly listened at the door and grasped the door knob to open it but stopped as I realized what I heard, a *prayer*.

Some of the words were too hard to understand but I made out a few.

"Heavenly Father…"

Then I heard groaning. Then I heard more words that I couldn't make out and some that I could make out.

"It's too much…please…I need to know your will…"

Then I heard more groaning.

Dad prayed so hard that it scared me. I'd never heard anyone pray like that before. It seemed to be full of sorrow. His loud groans drew me to listen more. After a minute or so I left the doorway a changed person. I never knew that people prayed that way. I wondered what caused him so much pain and grief in his life. Did he and Mom have some trouble that I didn't know anything about? Maybe he worried about the Christmas season? Or maybe *Weasel*? Then I wondered if I'd done something wrong that I didn't know anything about.

I couldn't help but remember all the times I'd disappointed him. For some reason, I seemed to always do the things that he told me not to do. Like the time when I was just about three years old and he'd laid his Gibson guitar down on the couch to go into another room. He warned me to be careful around it. As soon as he got out of my sight, I jumped on it and *busted it*. I don't know why I did it. Then I couldn't help but think about the time I drew all over the bathroom door with a permanent marker like the door was a big chalk board and the marker, a piece of chalk that I could erase when I finished and no one would ever know the difference. He never painted over the drawing. I guess he wanted me to remember what I did every time I had to go pee.

As I walked back to my bedroom, I glanced into the living room where my family watched television. At one end of the house they were laughing at some TV show and at the other end of the house Dad poured his soul out to God. I found it so strange. I crawled into bed thinking about it all and wondering why Dad felt so grieved.

He'd taught me to pray the Lord's Prayer and sometimes I'd pray with him beside his bed at night. He also taught us to pray for our food and I'd never forget it.

God is great.
God is good.
Let us thank Him
For our food.
Amen.

My thoughts on prayer were pretty simple, I realized. I never knew a person could pray *so deeply* with such emotion and sorrow. He sounded like a broken man.

Why did I suddenly feel so small in the world?

I thought about how we're really all just hanging on to a planet, dangling in space. I felt like a speck in the universe. God suddenly seemed much bigger to me than I ever imagined before. He was much more than a baby in a manger. I always imagined God somewhere out past the stars but after hearing Dad pray that night, I realized God is much closer than I ever figured Him to be.

He's close enough to hear us pray.

Chapter Four
Saved in the nick of time

The bus ride to school the next week gave me a chance to admire everybody's Christmas decorations, and the longing inside me just grew stronger and stronger. Nella sat in front of me and went on about the trees she saw in other people's houses.

"Look at that one!" She laughed and pointed out a skinny tree that seemed inferior to her. "Our tree is way bigger than that one. I bet they went out and cut it from their own back yard." She laughed again. "Our tree is from the store. It's always perfect." She waited for me to agree with her but I didn't.

"I like Christmas trees that are *real* even if they're skinny." I kept on staring out the school bus window as I said it but could see the look on her face out of the corner of my eye.

"You don't even have a tree so how would you know!" She huffed and turned around and faced the front of the bus. For half a second I thought about telling her about my Christmas tree on old man Gibson's property but remembered the secret with Ruthie and changed my mind. I couldn't wait to get to school and see the real trees in the classrooms.

Nella whipped out a paperback book and read as fast as she could. We ignored each other the rest of the way to school.

When the bus stopped at Shirley School I realized how much I loved my school. I dreaded when it would be time to go to town school. The day grew closer and I could already feel it coming. It would happen when I went into the fifth grade. Then I figured all the fun would be over and I'd be sitting outside underneath the big tree ignoring the bell just like my oldest brother.

When he went into the fifth grade, he couldn't seem to adjust to town school. He sat under the big tree out in front of the school and wouldn't go in when the bell rang. He just kept sitting there like he didn't even hear the bell. Like the ringing bell wasn't really for him but just for all of those town kids. The principal called Mom to tell her about it and together they finally figured out that he missed Shirley School. As time went by, he eventually grew to like his new school and I knew I'd feel the same way when I went to town school.

At Shirley School we got to have a lot of fun even though we did school work. The playground equipment begged us to come and play. There were swings, slides, a merry-go-round, and Yuke tires that we could climb on. One Yuke tire stood leaned up against a tree upright and the other tire laid out flat in front of it. We loved to climb on those tires and hide inside the one that lay on the ground. Inside that tire is where I got my first boyfriend, Ernie. His hair and eyes were dark with long eyelashes. His eyes twinkled at me when he smiled and I liked that. He held my hand as we sat together inside the big Yuke tire waiting for the bell to ring to go back to class. It only lasted a couple of days. I don't think he was ready for a girlfriend yet. I guess I wasn't ready for a boyfriend either. I figured that we'd get together again someday, but we never did.

I got off the bus and made my way to class.

Anna Lee rushed to me as soon as I stepped into our classroom and exclaimed, "I got saved last night!"

I immediately imagined that she fell into a river and nearly drowned just as someone reached and plucked her out just in the nick of time.

"Who saved you?" I asked aghast with wide eyes.

"The preacher!" She stated with certainty. Anna Lee's shoulder length brown hair bounced as she spoke. She beamed as I'd never seen before. Her teeth seemed whiter and her eyes brighter. She glowed with something new.

"The preacher saved you? Wow! What happened?" With the image of her nearly drowning still fresh in my mind, I waited anxiously for her to tell me about her near death experience and how the preacher saved her from drowning in the raging river.

Her story surprised me because instead of nearly drowning in a river, she began to tell me about being saved in church.

Church? I wondered. I went to church every Sunday and nobody ever *got saved* in my church. So I tried not to look confused and listened with great curiosity to what she said.

"I went up in front of the church and began to cry when the preacher reminded me that I was a sinner and told me how much I needed Jesus for forgiveness. He said that if I wanted to be saved from the fires of Hell that I needed to repent and ask Jesus to come into my heart. Then he prayed with me and I *got saved*! I asked Jesus to come into my heart and He did! I'm getting baptized pretty soon, too." Anna Lee smiled from ear to ear and I didn't ask any more questions because I realized that I didn't understand what happened to her. But I knew someone who would know so I waited until I got home to ask Dad.

When I walked into the house after school I saw Ruthie in the kitchen with Mom. She stood in a kitchen chair helping Mom stir something in a big bowl on the table. The aroma hit me and I could see that Mom went all out for dinner and made pies for dessert. She made baked chicken with dressing, mashed potatoes, corn, green beans and macaroni and cheese, along with her famous homemade yeast rolls. It was the macaroni and cheese that Ruthie stirred at the table.

Anytime Mom made pies, she went on ahead and made four or five which I found to be lucky for me because then I knew that I could have some of my favorite – lemon meringue. My older brother's favorite pie was coconut cream and my oldest brother always asked Mom to make him chocolate. Mom made them each their own special pie.

After dinner, Dad relaxed in his recliner with his well worn Bible in his lap lit up by the lamp next to him. He flipped through the thin pages of the Bible with calloused hands. That's where he could usually be found in the evenings after dinner. He preached at a small Primitive Baptist Church but he worked underground in the lead mines to support his large family. I watched him read and ponder God's word until it seemed that he finished studying and then I approached him with my burning question.

"Dad, what does *getting saved* mean?" I asked quietly. I told him about Anna Lee and her experience at church.

He nodded his head as I spoke and cleared his throat. Then he began to explain to me about "getting saved".

"Do you remember the story of Adam and Eve? How they disobeyed God in the Garden of Eden?"

I did.

"Well...because they sinned against God, then we, as their descendants, inherited that sin nature. Do you understand that?"

"Not really," I admitted. That sounded kinda complicated to me.

"Well...let me see if I can explain it in a better way." He thought for a moment and gently flipped the pages of his Bible with two fingers. Then he looked at me real serious and stared straight into my eyes. I swallowed as he began.

"Have you ever told a lie or done anything that you knew was *wrong*?" He smiled knowing good and well that I couldn't deny my guilt. I flashed back to the time I stole my sister Kate's gold baby ring from her jewelry box. It looked so nice on my ring finger and it fit me perfectly. So, I thought I should have it. Even though I gave it back a week after I took it cause Mom realized what I'd done. I was riddled with guilt over taking it in the first place. I still couldn't figure out how she knew that I took it. She always said there were eyes in the back of her head and she could see things we didn't think she could see. I guess that's how she knew.

Then memories flooded my mind with the many times I lied to get out of trouble. I thought about my artwork on the bathroom door and the busted guitar on the couch. My face burned hot with embarrassment as I recalled all my many sins.

"Yes," I quietly answered - full of shame and sorrow.

"That's what I'm talking about. You inherited a sinful nature. It's not your fault. We all have it. *That's why we need Jesus*. He came and lived a perfect life so that we could have a right relationship again with God. He died on the cross as a sacrifice for all our sins. It's only through Christ that your sins are forgiven and you will have eternal life."

He believed strongly in God's all-sufficient grace and finished with a strong but gentle statement.

"The preacher didn't save your friend. It was God. God saves us. Nobody else can do it - not even our selves. The Holy Spirit *draws us* and then we can be saved by God's grace."

A light bulb went off inside my head as I realized that people did get saved in my church - we just didn't call it that. So, getting saved *meant* following Jesus. *Oh.*

"Now, do you understand?" He asked me gently.

"I think so."

"When you feel the Holy Spirit drawing you, that's when you need to follow Jesus. That's how God arranged things." He smiled and went back to reading his scriptures.

Satisfied with his explanation, I thought about the baby Jesus in the manger and my solo. The next time I sang it I'd think real hard about what Jesus did for me on the cross and following Him. I'd listen to the Holy Spirit and see if He was *calling me.*

Chapter Five

A Sister's Christmas

"We're going to Elizabeth's house for dinner tonight," Mom informed us when we got home from school the next day.

I couldn't wait! My favorite older sister always fixed something good and even though she lived in a very small house we always had fun. She'd married a Free Will Baptist. He liked to corner Dad and ask questions about predestination and free will. Anytime I saw them talking away from everyone else I knew that if I listened long enough the conversation would become heated. My brother-in-law protested with a firm conviction that man possessed the free will to choose God or deny Him while Dad firmly believed that God chose His children before the foundation of the world and nothing could change that.

When he first started dating Elizabeth I decided right away that I didn't like him. For one thing, I could see that they really liked each other and maybe even loved each other and I didn't want things to change. I wanted Elizabeth to stay living at home with us just like I wanted my oldest sister to stay home when she got married. I didn't like things changing much. So, the more he came around and things got serious - the more I decided that I needed to try to like him if I could do it. But my disappointment showed in their wedding pictures because the frown on my face glared in every photo. Partly because I hated the shoes that Mom bought me to wear with the dress she made me but mostly because I didn't want Elizabeth to get married and move away even if it was just a mile up the street. Eventually, I accepted it and grew to like him a little more.

I went to my room and lay down on the bed. Ruthie busied herself playing with her dolls in the living room so I got the room to myself for a little while. I closed my eyes and relaxed. Soon I drifted to sleep. It seemed like only minutes before the door burst open.

"Our tree is ruined!" Ruthie cried out. She stood beside the bed looking like our dog just died. I sat up and tried to figure out what she was talking about.

"It's ruined!" Ruthie pointed out the window above the bed. I peeked out at the little pine tree across the fence. The pounding rain ruined our secret Christmas tree. The toilet paper looked like white mush and it didn't look like a Christmas tree anymore. I never considered the rain when we decorated it. A frown formed on my face that matched hers. She joined me looking out the window and I patted her back.

"It's all right, Ruthie. We'll figure out something else." A tear ran down her cheek and she wiped it with her sleeve.

"Girls, get your shoes on and go get in the car. It's time to go see your sister." Mom noticed Ruthie's tears and asked with genuine concern, "What's wrong?"

"Nothin'," I answered for Ruthie.

Mom looked out the window. When she spied the small, still slightly decorated pine tree, she asked, "Does this have something to do with that little tree I see?" Mom sighed. "Awe, it looks like someone's tree got all wet. I'm sorry girls, but you know how your daddy feels. We have to respect his convictions. It's just the way things are." She wiped Ruthie's tears and patted her blond head. "We're still going to have Christmas – just not the decorations." Mom smiled and kissed Ruthie on the forehead, "Now go get your shoes and let's get going."

I sulked.

Why did Christmas decorations have to be Dad's conviction? Why couldn't he be convicted about something else that I didn't care about? Everyone else seemed to have a Christmas tree. At least everyone I knew did. It just didn't seem fair.

We used to have a tree cause I remembered it. The tall cedar tree stood firm in a bucket full of rocks. Different colored lights sparkled within the branches of the tree. Tinsel danced from the branches and presents were stacked up underneath. The scent of cedar always reminded me of that one memory. *Why did Dad think it was wrong now?* I wondered.

I knew the answer even though I didn't like it. We kids, mostly me, asked him repeatedly over the years for a tree. He always answered, "You don't need a tree and decorations to celebrate Christmas." He hated the way the world made Christmas more about Santa Claus coming than baby Jesus coming.

When I turned two years old he changed churches. That's when we stopped having a Christmas tree. That's when he *got convicted*. I wished I could say that I understood why because he was the most spiritual person that I knew but I didn't understand. Neither did Ruthie. Although she never knew that we ever even had a tree because she wasn't born yet when I remembered us having one. She just thought it would be fun. I just wanted to celebrate Christmas like everyone else on our street. To me, a tree was a beautiful Christmas decoration.

Ruthie and I obeyed Mom and put our shoes and coats on. We piled into our station wagon and headed to Elizabeth's house. The rain continued to drizzle as we drove to her house behind the Missionary Baptist Church. Dad grew up in that church and we used to be members there. A lot of our extended family members were buried in the grave yard by the church. When my baby sister died they buried her there. Well, she was my older sister but a baby when she died. Her homemade cement headstone lay flat in the ground. Little bitty shells spelled out her name. Anne Marie. I loved her name even though I never met her. Some of the shells were missing on the headstone which made it difficult to read. But we all knew what it said and Mom planned on getting her a new one but hadn't done it yet. My sister died at three months old of crib death. Mom snapped a picture of her one day when she lay on their bed and I liked to look at it. She reminded me of Mom with her dark hair and dark eyes. I often wondered about her and what she would look like if she'd have gotten a chance to grow up like the rest of us. She would have been almost as old as Elizabeth. She died in my parents' bed one night and Dad wore himself sick thinking that maybe, while he slept, he'd accidentally rolled on top of her or something like that and she couldn't breathe. The doctor ruled it as crib death and *nothing else*. Still, it bothered him something terrible until he dreamed about her one night. She sat high upon a cloud and seemed happy as could be. Somehow, even though she was just a baby, she waved and smiled at him. After the dream, Dad felt comforted.

We passed the cemetery and drove down the driveway that led to my sister's house. The short ride ended and we piled out and went inside. The aroma of spaghetti and garlic bread wafted through the tiny house. It smelled delicious. My parents talked to my sister and brother-in-law while we kids went to admire her tree. The lights cast a soft glow over the small living room. It made the tree in my classroom seem like a sad little tree. All of the decorations were bought from the store. There were lots of white lights hidden within the branches that were laden down with shimmering gold balls and sparkling ribbons. Some of the ornaments were painted with different Christmas scenes. The angel lit up the top of the tree in a golden dress. She wasn't made from paper and glitter. I stared, mesmerized.

We settled down to dinner and Dad prayed over the food. His prayer touched me as he asked God to bless their home and my sister's family and of course, the food to the nourishment of our bodies. It seemed that Dad prayed with such depth that I wanted to do it, too. I remembered the prayer I overheard in his bedroom. Then he finished praying for the food with "Amen" and everyone started scarfing.

My little brother slurped down spaghetti. He shoved it into his mouth with *both* hands. A noodle slapped his nose as he sucked it down and laughter filled the house.

After dinner and the dishes were washed, Elizabeth reached under the tree and pulled out gifts for each of us. She gave Ruthie a baby doll. Then she handed me a gift and I tore it open, revealing a pink Barbie doll case.

"Look inside." Elizabeth encouraged me to open the case. I lifted the lid of the Barbie doll case and found it full of Barbie accessories that I longed for. Dresses, boots, blouses, pants, hair brushes and miniature doll furniture. I yelped with delight. I hugged her and she held me tight.

"Do you like it?" She winked at me. "Is it what you wanted?"

"Yes! I love it! Thank you Elizabeth!" I meant it, too.

"Good then Merry Christmas!"

By the time we were done unwrapping presents, crumpled paper covered her floor. Everyone admired their gifts as Elizabeth began to play the piano. The tree glowed and joy filled her house. I couldn't remember a more wonderful Christmas celebration and a pang of envy stung me as she played the piano that I loved and her beautiful tree lit up the room. I determined that someday I would have a Christmas like that when I got married and moved away.

When we got home I put my Barbie in the new case and kept it in bed with me. The plastic smell of the case and Barbie filled the room. I clung to it and nodded off to asleep only to be awakened by the sound of music coming from my parents' bedroom. *Music?* It sounded like an instrument.

I listened quietly as I held on to my Barbie case. It sounded like a piano. An impossible hope began to fill me. A piano? Was it possible that my parents hid a piano in their room for me for Christmas? My heart raced at the possibility as I listened to the music in the room next to mine.

Ping, ping, ping.

What in the world? I listened intently until finally it stopped and even Ruthie's thumb smacking couldn't stop the smile that spread across my face as I drifted off to sleep.

Chapter Six

A Christmas Story

My glamour queen sister fixed my hair for the Christmas program at school the next evening. My nerves were already about to get the best of me as I sat in a chair in front of the mirror in her bedroom. The top of her dresser was organized perfectly. A brush, comb and mirror were nicely laid out. Her jewelry box and bottles of perfume stood in front of the mirror and nail polish bottles were lined up neatly in a row.

She took strips of my straight hair and curled each tightly. By the time she finished, I almost looked as glamorous as her. She powdered my face and painted my lips pink. She pulled back a few front strands of curly hair and held them with a barrette. I couldn't believe how nice I looked all fixed up. She smiled at me and held up the mirror as she turned me around to view the back of my hairdo. I never looked so good in my whole life.

"Thanks!" I took another look at myself in the mirror hardly believing the lovely young girl I saw could be me.

"You're welcome. Good luck with your solo, squirt." She opened the bedroom door slowly and sang, "Here she is…Miss America!" She dramatically motioned her arm for me to walk out of the bedroom. I posed outside the door feeling very special.

"Doesn't she look great?" She asked expectantly while turning me around for everyone to see the full view of her handiwork.

"Oh, my goodness! She looks marvelous!" Mom exclaimed. Nobody ever referred to me as marvelous before that I could remember. I figured I must really look *good*.

My sister took a big bow and said, "My work here is done." She laughed then went back into her room to grab her coat.

"Time to go kids. Let's all head over to the school," Mom said while Dad started the car. We got on coats and shoes and loaded into the wagon.

"Oh, I almost forgot." Mom went into the kitchen and opened up the refrigerator. She pulled out a clear plastic box with a flower corsage inside. She opened it up and motioned for me to come closer.

"Isn't this lovely? It matches your dress." She pinned the corsage onto my dress and I felt even more beautiful. It was the first flower anyone ever bought me. The golden ribbon on it glittered and sparkled and I smiled. I proudly climbed into the station wagon. Ruthie stared at the corsage when I sat down beside her in the back of the car.

"Where's mine?" She asked with a frown forming on her face.

"You'll get one when you grow up a little, honey. It's a special night for Anna." Mom said over her shoulder from the front seat. Ruthie sulked.

My stomach churned with butterflies. *What had I gotten myself into?* The more I thought about singing in front of all of those people the more I decided that I didn't want to sing the solo. How could I get out of it?

I sat in the backseat of the wagon staring out the steamed up window. It seemed that Christmas trees glowed in the window of every house I saw. I couldn't wait to show Ruthie the tree in my classroom.

"Get over. You're on my side." My older brothers began to argue in the seat in front of me and Ruthie. "I'm sitting on the hump! You scoot over!" They pushed each other.

"Stop fighting! I don't want to hear another word! Do you understand me? I mean it!" Mom lost her temper. "Do you want Dad to pull this car over?"

"No," they both mumbled but continued to push at each other until we pulled into the school parking lot.

"Okay, everybody behave!" Mom meant it, too because she gave *the look* to everyone in the car. Then she smiled at me, "Good luck, honey. Sing sweet." I climbed out of the car and went to the classroom.

Mrs. Wise stood in the back of the line and helped us line up on the risers. Then the program began. My stomach wouldn't stop fluttering as I lined up with my classmates and I swallowed over and over cause my mouth got real dry. When I saw my family in the audience, my oldest sister, Kate, waved at me and sat down with the rest of my family. I didn't see *Weasel* though. Somehow I calmed down and prepared myself for my solo.

The program began and as we sang *We Three Kings*, the three wise men slowly walked up front to where Joseph, Mary and the baby Jesus were to the side of the risers. Then my time to sing the solo arrived. I stepped down the risers and walked down front when our music teacher began the introduction of the song. With the microphone in my hand, I began to belt out "Away in a Manger". I looked at the manger scene as I sang and thought about the baby Jesus. He was so much more than a baby it seemed to me. I sang out the last verse and smiled. I looked at the aluminum foil covered star dangling over the baby Jesus and it twinkled.

I wondered at the fact that Jesus grew up and became a man and never sinned. It reminded me of all of my own sins and how I wished I could just erase them all. *Jesus will forgive me*, I thought. *He died for me. He is the son of God*! I marveled at the thought and I became certain that the Holy Spirit was calling me. Then I decided...*Yes, I want to follow Jesus.*

My prayer came quick and I remembered the part that Anna Lee said about asking Him to come into your heart and so I did. I never wanted to sin again. Never.

Applause broke out as I made my way back up the risers and my heart grew full with something that I didn't recognize. A warm feeling came over me as I looked at the manger scene. I'd never see it the same way again. The baby faded and He became a King. Right there in front of everyone, the Holy Spirit called me and I followed Jesus. I was a Christian. I was forgiven.

After the program, I found my family in the audience. I gave my pregnant sister a big bear hug.

"I'm so proud of you, Sissy! You did a great job!" She hugged me tight and I felt of her large belly. The baby kicked my hand and I smiled up at her. I didn't ask about *Weasel*.

"Thanks. I was really nervous though." I admitted.

"You couldn't tell," she reassured me.

Ruthie tugged on my sleeve because she wanted to go see our class tree. So I took her to my classroom so that she could see all the decorations our class made.

"Wow. It's so pretty." She stared, mesmerized by its beauty as it sparkled in the dark classroom.

"See these snowflakes?" I pointed out a snowflake that we'd cut out in class. "This is how they're supposed to turn out."

"Oh, I see." She studied the snow flakes and then took to admiring the sparkling sequined balls hanging from the tree.

Daniel and his brother came into the classroom followed by their little sister holding his mother's hand. Daniel showed his family the tree we decorated, too. His brother and sister seemed as impressed as Ruthie. His mother didn't say much. She looked a lot like Daniel. She reached up and touched a snowflake with a thin, frail hand. Her hands looked like she washed a lot of dishes to me or else she did a lot of work around the house.

"Hello," I said to Daniel's mom and she nodded at me with a slight smile.

"Hello," she said and then as almost an afterthought, "I liked your solo."

"Thanks!" I gleamed and she nodded at me and then went back to looking at the tree with Daniel's brother and sister.

I wanted to say something else to her but didn't know what to say so I just grabbed Ruthie's hand and we roamed the other classrooms checking out all of the other Christmas trees. Finally, the crowd began to disperse and so our family headed home, too. My pregnant sister climbed into the car with us and I was puzzled. One of my older brothers squeezed into the back with Ruthie and me to make room in the station wagon for her to ride. Nobody said anything about it so I didn't either. When we got home Mom got out blankets for her and she rested on the couch with a pillow propping up her head.

After everyone fell asleep that night, I overheard them talking in the living room. I couldn't make out everything but I figured out that *Weasel* continued living up to his secret nickname and my sister needed to get away for awhile. It made me so angry. Mom and Dad said she could stay for as long as she wanted to. I hoped she would move back in with us. Then we could dance again in the living room with the radio blaring like nobody's business. It was one of our favorite things to do. She taught me how to do a funny dance called the *Funky Chicken*. I missed her. I missed her living at our house. It seemed she didn't come around much anymore. (Probably because of *Weasel*.) I decided that I didn't like him much either.

Ruthie smacked her thumb and I tried to go to sleep but I kept thinking about the Christmas program and then about my pregnant sister's situation. I thought about Dad's prayer that I'd overheard and wondered if maybe this is what he prayed so hard about? Maybe he knew more about *Weasel* than the rest of us knew. I couldn't help but wonder about *Weasel* and why he seemed so bad. His parents were God fearing Christians and raised him up the best way they knew how. Once, Mom told me that *Weasel's* older brother was a vegetable.

"What do you mean a vegetable?" I asked in astonishment when I imagined a big squash or zucchini lying on a bed.

"It means that he's in a coma. He's in a deep sleep and he's not gonna come out of it."

"Why?" I asked Mom. Relief washed over me when I realized he wasn't a real vegetable from the garden.

"Well, he was in a real bad car accident one night and he got hurt real bad. His brain got damaged. The doctors couldn't fix it so now he will live the rest of his life in a bed hooked up to machines." Mom sighed and lowered her gaze then said, "It's sad."

"Can he get up to go to the bathroom?" I asked curious how in the world that would work.

"No. They have him hooked up to go to the bathroom." Mom looked at me curiously and then said, "It's like he's sleeping, Anna...but he can't wake up."

The thought of that made me sad. "Never?" I asked.

"I don't think so. The doctors don't think so either," she answered.

I figured that might explain why *Weasel* couldn't be nice to Kate. *Maybe he's upset about his brother's coma condition.* I thought.

"Is *Weasel* mad about his brother?" I asked.

"Oh, I don't know about that." Mom sighed and then looked at me real serious. "The truth is that *Weasel* was driving the car the night of the accident. I'm sure he's having a hard time with knowing that he was behind the wheel when his brother was put into that condition. I don't think there's anything that he could have done different that night though if you ask me. It was just a terrible accident. Another car crashed right into the side of them and there was no way to avoid it. No one blames him that I know of. So, maybe he blames himself but he shouldn't."

Mom smiled at me and pushed my bangs away from my eyes. She bent down and kissed me on the forehead. Then finished with, "that's no excuse for the way he acts. He needs to lay off the liquor some. That would help."

"Oh," was all that I could think to say when Mom said that. We never talked about it again.

I rolled around in bed thinking about it all. What would it be like not to be able to wake up? It sounded awful to me. Could he hear people talking to him? Did he want to answer and just couldn't speak? Once, I dreamed something like that. I tried and tried to wake up from the dream but I couldn't. It horrified me.

Then I remembered my new found relationship with Jesus and decided to talk to God before I went to sleep. Mostly to thank him for forgiving my sins but also for letting my sister stay with us again. I got out of bed and down on my knees like Dad taught me. Ruthie's stinky red socks were lying beside the bed so I picked them up and tossed them out the door and onto the kitchen floor so that I didn't have to smell them as I prayed. I prayed silently.

Dear God,

Thank you for making me a Christian and forgiving me and thank you for Jesus comin' and dying on the cross for all our sins. I'm sorry that I lied and stole my sister's ring from her jewelry box. Thank you for sending my sister to our house and please, God, take care of her and can you make Weasel be nice to her? Plus, can you help his brother wake up so he won't be a vegetable anymore? Please wake him up.

Please bless my family and protect us. Also, is there any way you could change Dad's mind about Christmas trees?

In Jesus' name,

Amen.

I got up off my knees and crawled into bed. I felt great comfort knowing God called me one of His children and I fell asleep real peaceful but later the phone rang and woke me up.

"Hello?" Mom answered groggily. I glanced at my alarm clock and it read three o'clock in the morning. *Who would call at this time of night?* Something terrible must have happened or someone died because no one ever called at that time of night for any other reason.

"Go ahead. You come right on over here and see what happens when you do!" Mom said in a tone reserved for her angriest moments at us kids.

"No. You're not talking to her right now. She's sleeping and you better not call here again at this hour unless someone is dead!" Mom slammed the phone down and my heart pounded like crazy. *Weasel!*

I feared that he'd come over and start making trouble. Mom went through the house checking all the doors to make sure they were locked. Dad got out of bed too and stood in the living room where my pregnant sister slept through the whole thing somehow. He pulled back the living room curtains and looked out the picture window to see if *Weasel* might really be coming or if he was just full of hot air as usual. Mom saw me peeking through the bedroom door.

"Go back to bed, Anna, everything's okay. He wouldn't dare come over here. He's just making threats. He's probably been drinking." She went back into her bedroom and I crawled back into bed. After awhile, I heard Dad go back to bed, too.

It seemed like hours that I laid there thinking about *Weasel*. Why couldn't he treat my sister better? Why did she fall in love with him and *marry* him? I secretly wished that she didn't. He seemed like such a jerk.

I thought about my prayer earlier that night. Maybe it didn't take.

Chapter Seven
Party time!

"Rise and shine! Rivulet! Hit the deck! Roll 'em out!" Mom made her way through the house with her morning wake up call. There were dark circles under her eyes and she seemed more tired than usual when she attempted to get us all up for school. Maybe she couldn't sleep either because of Weasel's phone call.

My pregnant sister, Kate, sat on the couch chomping down a bowl of cereal. I went to give her a hug. Her long, wavy, brown hair tickled my nose when I hugged her and she squeezed me tight.

"Hey Sissy." Nobody called me that except for her.

"Did you sleep okay?" she asked me. It seemed that she didn't know Weasel woke us up in the middle of the night.

"I guess," I said because I finally I fell back to sleep after all of the thinking I did in the middle of the night.

"I slept like a rock. Even on this old couch!" She smiled and she didn't seem to know about the phone call and how worried Mom and Dad were in the middle of the night over her. I figured she knew *Weasel* best. Maybe she knew why he acted like he did and I guess she loved him anyway.

I suddenly remembered that we were having a Christmas party at Shirley School and I brightened up. I got dressed and ate as fast as I could because I couldn't wait to get to school. I kissed my pregnant sister's forehead on my way out the door to catch the bus but she stopped me. She held up her hand and pulled off a gold ring from her pinky. It was the little gold ring I'd stolen from her jewelry box a few years back.

"Here." She handed me the ring. "I want you to have this. It's too small even for my pinky now. Maybe it will fit you. I know you love it." She smiled at me and I slipped it onto the ring finger of my right hand. It fit me perfectly.

"Thanks." I looked down at the ring. I couldn't help but be reminded of my terrible sin as I stared at it. Then I remembered that God forgave me and a smile slowly spread across my face. It was the only thing I'd ever stolen and now Kate gave it to me free and clear.

"You're welcome." She pulled me to her and hugged my neck. "Consider it a Christmas present." Then she added, "Have a good day at school."

"I will! We're having a Christmas party!" I announced and headed to the bus stop.

I caught the bus like normal and ran inside the school building as soon as the doors of the bus opened. We sat in class and it seemed that the morning work would last forever because the party wouldn't start until after lunch. The presents were piled up underneath the tree and the excitement grew as we drudged our way through the daily grind. Bridget brought a whole plate full of cookies from the store with Santa Claus' face painted on each one with red and white icing. Anna Lee brought homemade reindeer candy canes and I couldn't wait to gobble one of those down, too. I brought a present for the teacher but no food for the party. It didn't matter to Mrs. Wise. She just wanted us all to have a great time.

Finally, lunchtime came and then the party began! Each kid in class brought a present for either a boy or a girl. They were the ones piled up underneath the tree. Mrs. Wise called us each by name and we got to go pick out any present we wanted. I felt sorry for the last person to get their name called because they always ended up with the smallest gift. I unwrapped my present and discovered a package of pretend nail polishes. Just what I always wanted!

"What did you get?" I asked Anna Lee as Jill stood alongside her wearing her gift. A shiny gold bracelet dangled on Jill's small wrist. Anna Lee held up a puzzle with a goofy smile on her face. *A puzzle?* I thought pretend nail polishes were much better. Anna Lee shrugged, "At least the puzzle is cute little kittens!" Those were her favorite.

"Look!" I held out my nail polishes. We tore open the package they were sealed up in then sat across from each other and painted each other's nails.

Daniel sat at his desk in front of us holding a small globe. He spun it with his finger and stared until it stopped spinning. Then he spun it again. He looked around to see if anyone noticed him. I caught his eye and went to see his globe when the fingernail polish dried on my nails.

"Can I see it?" I asked.

He handed the globe to me and I examined it carefully. It looked like a perfect miniature of the Earth.

"This is where we are." He pointed to our state on the globe.

"Cool." I spun it again and handed it back to him. He smiled at me and it seemed to be the first time I'd ever seen him smile. It made him look handsome. I think he liked his globe.

Mrs. Wise opened the gifts on the top of her desk. They'd accumulated into a tall stack. There were bottles of perfume, soaps and bath cubes. She seemed thrilled with each gift. My gift was a small bottle of perfume that Mom purchased from the Avon lady. I thought it smelled nice.

"Thank you so much, kids!" She expressed her gratitude with a big smile.

"It's time to go. Line up, please."

We lined up and headed into the cafeteria then sat down to receive a brown paper bag full of goodies. The brown paper bag contained an orange, an apple, some hard candy, a candy cane, some nuts and a chocolate crème drop. The principal of our school made sure that each child got a gift.

One child, Jack, got some special gifts because he wasn't like the rest of us somehow. The principal bought him new tee shirts, underwear, long sleeve shirts and socks. Usually, Jack came to school dressed in old worn-out clothes. Almost every day he ran around chasing everyone yelling at the top of his lungs. When he ran around for very long, his breathing changed. He took short hard breaths and inhaled real deep when he laughed like it took his breath away. He smiled a lot like he'd just gotten away with something that none of the rest of us knew anything about. Most of us liked to get chased by him around the playground or gym. But sometimes he'd scare someone and they would run and tell the teacher. She'd make him sit down for a few minutes but as soon as he got back up he'd start chasing everyone again. I don't know why he enjoyed it so much. We all loved him none the less.

The party finally ended and we gathered up our treasures and headed to the buses. Anna Lee and I were walking out together when I heard my name.

"Anna, come here please." Mrs. Wise stood by the classroom door. Anna Lee went on out to the buses and I ran back to the classroom. Mrs. Wise handed the paper angel to me from the top of the classroom tree. I stared at the beautiful paper angel with my mouth hanging open.

"I thought you might like this." She smiled and her dark eyes smiled, too, as she handed me the lovely paper angel.

"Thanks Mrs. Wise!" I held the angel in my hands like she was made of china instead of paper and couldn't wait to show it to Ruthie. Christmas break, finally!

When the bus dropped me off I ran into the house to see my pregnant sister, Kate, only to discover she already left. She'd gone back to *Weasel*. My heart sank when Mom told me because I wanted everything to be the way it used to be. I wanted us to do the *funky chicken* and have fun again dancing to the radio. I wished we could run away together again like we did once when Mom wouldn't let me wear a dress that I loved. She'd said I could only wear it for special occasions.

Kate said she'd run away with me if I wanted her to when she saw me sitting outside crying over it. I perked up because it sounded like a good way to get back at Mom for not letting me wear the dress. So, she held my hand and we walked a mile away to the creek where we kids swam every summer. We spent a whole day there. We waded in the cool, rippling creek water. Then caught crawdads and skipped rocks until finally I got pretty hungry.

"I'm hungry," I whined.

"I didn't bring anything to eat," she answered. Then she looked at me and smiled as a thought crossed her mind. "We can eat some crawdad tails." Kate started gathering up little sticks to start a fire with.

"Yuck. I don't want to eat crawdad tails." I scrunched up my nose at the thought.

"Well, that's good because I forgot to bring ketchup." She laughed as she tossed the sticks into the air and I didn't care about the dress anymore. We went home and Mom never said a word about it.

Nothing like that could ever happen again because there's no going backwards and no making things the way they used to be. She was married and expecting a baby. Kate had a new family.

Chapter Eight
What's Inside

The next morning I opened my eyes to the beautiful sight of snow piling up outside. Everything looked bright and new. It was coming down like crazy. The flakes were big and fluffy and I could make out the intricate detail of a snowflake stuck to my bedroom window seal. I marveled at it as it slowly disappeared as another flake landed on top of it and then another.

"Wake up!" I shook Ruthie to wake her.

She moaned and rolled over in bed sucking her thumb enthusiastically.

"It's snowing!" I shook her again.

This time she sat up and jumped to the window. Those big brown eyes smiled and she jumped up and down on the bed.

"Let's go!" I said and we both started piling on clothes to go outside and play. We bundled up with two pair of socks, sweatpants with blue jeans over them, tee shirts with flannel shirts over them, a sock cap and gloves and to finish it off, a coat and scarf. We crammed our pant legs into boots and headed outside.

Nella waltzed down the road toward our house pulling her sled behind her. When we got outside and into the front yard, she waved and trudged up our driveway. Our front yard sloped by the fence and so the sledding began. Of course, Nella controlled who could ride because she owned the sled. After a few runs down the hill, Ruthie and I decided to find something we could ride on without being bossed around by Nella. We searched behind our house but there were no sleds back there. We did find a big piece of metal that looked like it would go down the hill nicely. So, we drug it to the front yard and piled on. We rode it down the hill and it turned around in circles as it went which made the ride all the more exciting!

We rode sleds, ate snow, threw snowballs, and built a fort and a snowman until we were nearly frozen to death. Our fingers were beet red and we couldn't feel our toes.

We went inside the house and took off our snowy clothes by the door. The wood stove gave off a lot of heat so we laid our wet gloves and socks on top of it to dry them out quickly. The house was full of kids. Dad got off work because of the weather and sat in the recliner playing the guitar. My older brothers were sitting on the couch with my littlest brother sandwiched in between them. Mom busied herself cleaning up the kitchen with my glamour queen sister helping out. We warmed our hands and feet by the stove and the numbness slowly began to fade.

Dad strummed the guitar and started to sing a song. We knew the song well and hated it.

"*Mama, don't leave me. Please Mama don't go.*" He looked at us with a spark of mischief in his eyes and sang the sad tear jerker about a mother who leaves her child at home alone. Ruthie begged him to stop because she hated the way the song ended but he wouldn't because he loved to torment us with it. A smile crossed his face and he continued to belt out the heartbreaking song until the terrible ending when the baby in the song died of a broken heart. By that time all of us girls were hiding in my glamour sister's bedroom, holding back tears.

He loved to sing old tear-jerkers like that one to make us cry. When he finished, he would always sing some silly song to cheer us up again like the one where the cat gets caught in the washing machine or the song about the hotrod Ford racing the Model T down the highway and we'd all sing along with him. We loved it when he sang the song *I wish I was single again*! Or else he sang *There's a Hole in the Bottom of the Sea*. Our whole family knew all of the words and most of the neighbor kids did, too. He had *quite* a repertoire.

Above all of his lovely torments was to slowly begin to sing *I'm in the mood for love*. Every time he sang it we'd run and hide because it meant that he was coming after us and wasn't going to stop singing until he caught us wherever we were hiding and smothered us with kisses and rubbed his whiskers all over us. He finished the song as he tickled us until we could hardly stand it anymore!

He began to sing again and we went back into the living room and plopped down in front of the recliner to listen.

"She's got a freckle on her butt... but she's pretty!" He strummed the guitar and sang the song he'd made up about Ruthie's birthmark and we all busted out laughing. Ruthie smiled and her eyes gleamed with pride because Dad wrote her a song.

After several songs, our clothes were dried out enough on the stove to go back outside. We left Ruthie at home and headed to Nella's house to ride sleds because her yard turned into one giant hill with trees everywhere. After several runs down the hill we tuckered out though because getting back up the hill wasn't worth the thrill of flying down it anymore.

"Let's go inside and have some hot chocolate," she suggested. I gladly agreed.

When we stepped inside her house I saw it - her glorious Christmas tree. The big fake tree was very nice. I couldn't claim it to be the most beautiful tree I'd ever seen because that tree stood in my sister's living room in the little house behind the Missionary Baptist Church. She smiled.

"I like your tree," I said and reached up to touch a delicate decoration.

"*Don't!* You're going to break that!" She pushed my hand away. "That's an heirloom decoration handed down from my Great Grandmother!"

"Oh. Sorry." How in creation could I possibly know that? I really didn't know much about decorations being as I didn't have any of my own.

Her mood changed immediately as she said, "Let me plug in the lights." She bent under the tree and plugged the electric cord into the outlet.

"There!" She stood proudly with her hands on her hips as her tree sparkled to life. Then she thought for a second and said, "When we open presents on Christmas morning each kid has a different kind of wrapping paper. That's how we know which present is our*s*!" She informed me.

"Neat." I nodded but wished she'd have kept it to herself. I didn't need to hear about her fabulous Christmas traditions. Especially, since my family didn't have any.

"This is your present," she sang and reached under the tree pulling out a small box wrapped in shiny blue paper with a silver bow on top. There was my name right on the official nametag.

I reached inside my coat pocket and pulled out a present for her. Mom picked it up at the store for me after a good deal of leg scratching took place. I wrapped it in thin red and green paper with snowmen on it. We were out of scotch tape so I used masking tape. There wasn't a bow on it because Ruthie and I tore them all apart making Christmas tree decorations for our tree on old man Gibson's land. I made a homemade nametag by folding over a piece of wrapping paper and writing her name on the inside. She didn't seem to mind my wrapping job as she swapped presents with me. She looked at the masking tape and busted out laughing. I went to laughing too because even though I did my best wrapping job on the present - it was funny.

We sat down and opened them in front of her tree. (It felt a little like Christmas to me.) Nella bought me a birthstone necklace. The amethyst stone sparkled in the light. I watched her open hers and she pulled out a silver charm bracelet with the Ten Commandments dangling from it. She smiled and I helped her put it on. Then she clasped the necklace around my neck. We went to admire ourselves in her bedroom mirror.

She hugged my neck awkwardly and said, "Thank you!"

"Thanks! I love my necklace." I admired its beauty in the mirror.

"Hot chocolate?" Nella asked grinning at me in the mirror.

"Yeah." I loved hot chocolate.

We sat at the kitchen table sipping on cups of hot chocolate with mini-marshmallows melting in the top of the cup. I sucked down the foamy marshmallows while she spooned hers into her mouth. When we were almost done she made a thoughtful suggestion.

"How about I take a picture of you in front of my Christmas tree?" She looked at me. I tried to figure out what she meant. At first I thought she was trying to rub her Christmas tree in my face again but then I realized that she wanted to share her Christmas tree with me.

"Okay." I smiled with melted marshmallows on my lips.

"I'll be right back." She went into the den and came back with her father's instant Polaroid camera. She motioned me into the living room.

I followed her and posed in front of the tree.

"Smile! Say CHEESE!" She clicked a photo while I gave my best smile. Then we waited for the picture to develop. Finally, I could see myself standing next to her glorious tree. My eyes were closed but they were almost always closed in photos because I blinked every time the flash went off.

"Here, Anna." She handed it to me. "Merry Christmas!"

I guess she got the Christmas spirit. It was just about the nicest thing she ever did for me that I could remember. Maybe I'd try and be a better friend to her. I really never tried very hard.

Then I bundled up and headed back to my house. It looked like a blizzard outside and I took to imagining that I got lost somewhere in the wilderness as I walked the familiar stretch of road home. As I walked down the road I saw something move out of the corner of my eye. I looked intently in the direction of the movement and saw someone standing behind a tree, hiding in the field next to the road. The snow just about blinded me but I thought I could make out someone moving. I turned and kept walking in hopes that they'd ignore me like I tried to ignore them. But then my head jerked forward real hard as something pelted me in the back of the head.

"Hey!" I yelled in the direction of the tree they used for cover. Then out jumped *Buster*.

"Hey yourself!" He sneered. In his hands he held two hard packed snow balls. I could tell how hard they were cause he kept pounding them in his hands and adding more snow as he started chasing me down the road. I ran as fast as I could as he continued to pelt me. I just about started to cry because the snowballs were so hard and he used all his force when he threw them at me. Then I saw my two older brothers coming up the road toward me. I was never so glad to see them in my life! One brother blocked me as tears welled up in my eyes and my oldest brother took to chasing Buster.

"You got nerve going after a little girl!" He yelled as he chased him down and pulled him to the ground. My other brother told me to go to the house and then he heaped on top of Buster, too. I don't know exactly what happened that day but Buster never bothered me again. I gained some new respect for my brothers too. I knew they'd protect me and that deep down somewhere they loved me.

Chapter Nine
That Little Old Church

When I woke up the next morning, I smelled fried chicken. Even though snow piled up to half a foot, we were still going to church. We girls still wore a dress and Mom still packed food for lunch after church. She woke up early and fried some chicken, made potato salad and her famous chocolate cake. The aroma of food woke us up that cold Christmas Eve morning instead of her usual morning call. Nothing wakes up the senses like good ole' fried chicken.

A line soon formed outside the bathroom door because we only had one. Ruthie hadn't wet the bed so she danced in place and tried not to pee her pants.

"I gotta go!" She yelled outside the bathroom door. I stood behind her waiting my turn and heard the faucet turn on as Dad washed his hands.

"He's almost done!" I told her.

Then finally the door opened and Dad came out wearing a blue suit. His slicked down hair looked real nice and a hint of Old Spice hung in the air. Then we smelled a hint of something else!

"Smells like roses!" He proudly announced and smiled as he left the bathroom so Ruthie could go. She turned her nose up in the air and held it with her two fingers.

"That stinks!" She took a deep breath of fresh air as she dodged into the bathroom.

Dad said the main roads were clear. He'd already driven to the main highway in his four wheel drive truck to check them out. We all got dressed and loaded into the station wagon. He backed out the slippery driveway with a car full of kids and Mom's hair full of rollers. We headed to church an hour away.

Mom dabbed Vanilla Musk behind her ears, put lipstick on and pulled rollers from her hair while Dad drove us into town. She fluffed her hair with her fingers as Dad pulled into his favorite donut shop at the top of the hill in town. Mom bought donuts and coffee for the road. The smell of donuts, coffee, Old Spice and fried chicken made me feel like throwing up. I thought I might barf. Ruthie opened up the lid on the fried chicken in the back and the smell was horrible. I lay down in the back of the station wagon and tried to block out the odors wafting around in the car.

We finally pulled into the parking lot of that little country church that had been my church for almost my entire life. It said PRIMITIVE BAPTIST CHURCH above the front door which stayed locked except during associations. We all scooted in through the kitchen door around back. Brother Pete lived just down the road from the church on a farm with lots of cattle. He always unlocked the church, got the gas stoves going and turned on the water in the well house before anybody else arrived for Sunday morning services.

"Good morning!" Brother Pete said in his usual upbeat manner as he handed each of us kids a piece of Dentyne gum. He shook all of our hands and welcomed us into the church. His wife, Sister Velva and her sisters met everyone with a hug. The gas stove in the kitchen and the stove in the main part of the building were kicked up on high. A rocking chair sat by the stove in the back of the church behind the pews. I sat down in it and warmed myself by the stove. I looked around at the little plain church that I loved so much. A bouquet of flowers always graced the table in front of the pulpit and songbooks were piled up there in a neat stack. A fresh glass of water sat on the edge of the table for the preacher to drink when he got thirsty during the sermon. The only picture on the wall revealed a brook dabbling along through a forest. There were two bathrooms in the back of the church - one for men and one for women. Once I'd accidentally opened up the door of the women's restroom while one of the older women still sat on the toilet. After that, I was sure to knock on the door before I charged in.

Sometimes preachers got so caught up in their sermons that I found it difficult to make out what they were saying. They called it *being in the spirit.*

During associations there were several preachers preaching for days. The preaching started on Friday night. Then, after we ate breakfast on Saturday morning, the preaching started again. We'd take a break for lunch and then they'd preach some more. Then we ate dinner and then more preaching. On Saturday night, some of the visitors would spend the night at church members' houses. Then we'd all get to church again Sunday morning for breakfast, and then there would be more preaching. Finally, after lunch on Sunday, the association ended. Mom didn't seem too sad about it because she could finally stop cooking.

Sometimes the associations were held at sister churches outside under a tent. It never failed to be in August and terribly hot. The best part of associations for me seemed to be that there might be some new kids there to play with. During the first service, I spent most of the sermon on the lookout for kids my age who might want to play after the service and maybe become friends. One time I thought I fell in love. The boy sat beside his younger brother and both shared the trademark dark hair and dark eyes that I found so attractive at my tender age. He spotted me and smiled. I looked down at my sandals and fidgeted with the saw dust scattered underneath my feet. When I looked again he held the stare and heat rose up my body to my face and burned red. After the last song ended and the invitation to join the church was offered with no new members and Brother Pete said a nice prayer, I hung around for a few minutes until he sauntered over to me and Ruthie.

"Hi there," he said and smiled.

"Hey," I said back and blushed again. Ruthie pulled on my hand to come see what was cooking for lunch. I nudged her to leave me alone and she grinned when she realized why.

"You from around here?" he asked.

"No, well I guess, sort of," came my uncertain answer. "I live about an hour away." I finally smiled and laughed at myself.

"Oh. I'm from Kentucky." He smiled and laughed, too.

"Kentucky?"

"Yes. It took us about six hours to get here," he answered and I thought he must have been bored coming all the way from Kentucky. It seemed like a long way from Missouri.

My brothers came up and joined the conversation.

"She's in third grade," they informed him and then looked at me and grinned. They loved to get my goat and I hated them at that moment for ruining the conversation with my dreamboat. Ruthie finally pulled me away and I went with her because before I knew it the boys were all talking about cars and motorcycles and drew his attention away from me. It didn't stop me from dreaming about him all through the services though.

I thought for sure that if we were destined to be together then one day we would be. We exchanged addresses before the end of the last service and about a week later I wrote him a letter. He wrote me back but I never received another letter after that. Kentucky seemed very far away to me but that just made it more romantic. In the end, it didn't work out because I never saw him again.

Dad and my brothers carried the food into the church and set it on the kitchen counter. Everyone talked about the snow and weather until singing time came. It was my favorite part of the church service. Anyone could request a song to sing. If you were quick enough to call out your number before anyone else did then your song would be chosen to sing next.

I had a plan for that glorious Christmas Eve morning. Inside my heart I yearned to sing a Christmas carol. I couldn't remember ever singing one in church. It seemed to me that most of my Christmas celebrating took place at Shirley School. Christmas at my church was just like any other Sunday - singing, preaching, good folks and food.

Usually, I always chose the same song *That Little Old Church*, Number 402 in the *Old School Hymnal*. So, while the singing commenced I searched the song book for a Christmas carol. I flipped through the pages. There didn't seem to be any. *Where are all of the Christmas carols?* I wondered. Time was passing me by and frantically I searched through the list of songs in the index until finally I found one. It seemed to be the only Christmas carol in the entire *Old School Hymnal*.

"Number 117!" I yelled out before they finished singing the song they were on. I knew I needed to be quick if I wanted to beat everyone else and get my song chosen.

"Number 117," I announced again more quietly when they were finished with the last verse of *Glorious Things of Thee Are Spoken*. Dad looked up number 117 and I saw a funny little smile spread across his face.

"Okay, Anna." He cleared his throat, "*Joy to the World*, Number 117."

He waited until everyone found the page number in the book and then he cleared his throat again, hummed a note or two and then led the song and I sang out as loud as I could.

Joy to the world, the Lord is come.

Let earth receive her King.

Let every heart prepare Him room

And Heaven and nature sing,

and heaven and nature sing,

and heaven and heaven and nature sing!

My older brothers were singing, too. Usually, they sat through church like they were sitting through a funeral. But they knew this song and they were singing almost as loud as me! Ruthie sang and beamed with joy. My glamour queen sister sang perfect alto and so I joined her on the lower part blending together beautifully. Mom smiled as she sang soprano with my little brother clapping his hands sitting on her lap. We finished out the last verse. It was the best I ever sang except maybe when I sang my solo in the school play. My heart really yearned for Christmas.

And then the preaching began. We kids had a hard time listening for very long because most of the sermons were somewhat over our heads. Then from time to time a visiting preacher would *get in the spirit*. Then we couldn't make out what he said either. But I picked up a valuable piece of information here and there. Saved by grace…God is sovereign…Jesus died on the cross for our sins. (I knew all about that one alright. Recently, I received forgiveness.)

The preaching lasted about an hour. By the time the preacher stopped preaching, stomachs were growling and Mom passed out papers and pens to most of us to keep us occupied. Dad made one pass to the back of the church during his sermon to flip my two older brothers on the head for fighting.

Dad offered an invitation and I started to go up front and announce that I made the decision to *follow Jesus* but fear got the best of me and I decided to wait and talk about it with Dad first. We finished up with *Amazing Grace* and the right hand of fellowship. That's when everyone in the church shook one another's hand or gave them a hug at the end of service. I went around and shook hands and got hugs from the other members. We ended with a prayer and then everyone headed to the kitchen for lunch.

The women busied themselves warming up dishes and cooking rolls. I helped make some tea and poured it into glasses over ice. The dessert table held numerous delicious looking dishes. The long buffet counter overflowed with different kinds of foods.

Finally, someone offered a prayer to bless the food and everyone filled their plates. I piled my plate with meatloaf, mashed potatoes, corn, a deviled egg and a buttered roll and went to sit at the kids table. Somehow we were all divided up. Men were at one table, women at another and then all the kids at another table.

When it was time to leave everyone hugged and said goodbye.

"Merry Christmas!" I heard some say as we piled into the car and drove the hour back home. Something about church just made me feel good inside.

Chapter Ten

From The Outside Looking In

When we got home from church Mom got a phone call.

"Oh! That's *just* awful." she gasped. Then she listened intently to whoever delivered the terrible news on the other end of the phone line. "Goodness gracious! That's terrible."

Pause.

"I don't even know what to say." Mom continued to listen.

Pause.

I listened carefully to see if I could figure out who the conversation concerned. I worried for a moment that it might be *Weasel*.

"Thanks for letting us know. We'll make a dish and take it over for the family. Goodbye." Mom sighed as she hung up the phone. I knew what taking food over for the family meant.

Someone's dead.

Any time someone died, neighbors and friends fixed food and took it to their house. Who died? I wondered.

Later that afternoon I found out who it was but never how or why. After hearing bits and pieces of different conversations, I figured out that my classmate Daniel's mother had taken her own life. I couldn't believe it. I just saw her at the Christmas program at school and she seemed fine. She even said hello to me. I found it hard to believe that she'd gone downhill that fast. I didn't understand.

"Why would she take her own life?" I asked Mom.

"I don't know, honey. Some people get depressed - especially around Christmas time." She sighed as she baked a lemon pie to take over to their house before we went to Grandma's house that night. I accepted her answer because I truly believed she didn't know why.

So I went to my room and shut the door. I lay down on the bed to think about it all. I remembered how much I envied the decorations on their house. The lights on the gutters and trees along with that wonderful lit up Santa face hanging on their door. (Not to mention their lovely Christmas tree.) Their home seemed so happy to me from the outside looking in. I remembered my friend, Daniel. My heart hurt for him. Poor Daniel.

Around Christmas time is when some people take their own lives? I pondered Mom's response. I thought Christmas time was the happiest time of the year. Why would someone be sad at Christmas time? It couldn't be because she didn't celebrate Christmas. I'd seen all of her lovely decorations.

It was the first time I ever knew that a person could take their own life. I couldn't imagine why she'd want to. What could be so terrible? Plus I couldn't imagine how she'd do it. I imagined that she jumped into a frigid lake or river and just didn't swim. The image frightened me.

I figured most folks died that way ever since I almost drowned the summer before in Pine Tree Lake. My older brother swam up behind me and ducked me in water over my head. I panicked because I couldn't go under without holding my nose and I'd just learned how to dog paddle. The water gushed into my nose and I sucked it into my throat. I flailed my arms as I tried to reach the surface for a breath and luckily, my glamour queen sister and my cousin jumped in and pulled me from the lake. I surely would have drowned that day if they hadn't have saved me - I'm sure of it.

I wanted to save Daniel's mom but it was too late for that. I thought about God and how He knows everything. Why didn't He save her? Why didn't He stop her? Didn't He know her children's hearts would be broken on Christmas day?

I decided to talk to Him about it. I got down on my knees beside my bed.

Dear God,

I heard about Daniel's mom taking her life today. I don't understand. Why, God? What made her so sad?

I know You know everything and I realize that You're in control. Dad says that You're sovereign. Why didn't You stop her? Why did You let this terrible thing happen on Christmas Eve? I don't understand.

I guess I just want to ask you to help Daniel get through this the best way he can. I know he is terribly sad right now. Please help him, God. Help all of them.

I guess that's all I wanted to say. Thanks for listening.

In Jesus' name,

Amen.

I sat on my bed and wondered why my prayers weren't taking. It seemed that *Weasel* was still a weasel and his brother was still a vegetable. Plus Dad still hadn't changed his mind about us having a Christmas tree. Maybe I wasn't praying right. Maybe my prayers weren't fancy enough for God. He was the God of everything. Maybe

He wanted me to pray to Him using *thee* and *thou* and whatnot. I didn't think I'd be very good at talking that way. All I knew was to talk to Him like I was talking to Dad or Mom. I figured God would like me to pray no matter how I said it. I guess sometimes God says no and you just don't hear Him plain.

On our way to Grandma's house to open gifts that evening we stopped by Daniel's house to drop off the lemon pie Mom baked for them. We pulled into their driveway and Dad carried the pie to their house. Daniel opened the door and the lit up Santa face swished back and forth a little. There was a feeling inside of me that I didn't like. I couldn't figure out what it was. Was it dread? Sadness? Daniel's dad stood behind him with his hand settled on Daniel's shoulder. He talked briefly with Dad. Daniel saw me in the back of the station wagon and waved. I waved back then took to looking at their decorations again. They didn't seem the same to me anymore.

Chapter Eleven
A Grandma's Gift

My Grandparents owned about thirty acres. Dad spent most of the summers there on a tractor tilling up the ground for a garden because he dreamed of owning a farm. Our house sat on an acre of ground so he enjoyed helping take care of my Grandparents' farm.

He planted corn every year on their land and it became torture to me. In his great desire to farm and work the land, he wanted to teach us to appreciate the land in the same way he did. So, he toted us all to the farm and showed us how to plant corn - *never ending rows of corn.* He tilled the ground and got it ready for planting and then each of us kids grabbed a handful of corn from the bucket. He proudly held up the kernel of corn and told us what to do.

"Now, dig a little hole with your big toe, like this." He showed us how to move the soft tilled dirt with his big toe. "Then drop two or three kernels into the hole and cover it up with dirt. Take three more steps and do it again." He smiled and left us each in a row to plant corn. I dreaded springtime because I knew we were doomed to plant corn on Grandpa and Grandma's farm. Luckily, it was Christmas time and not springtime.

Dad pulled into their driveway and parked the car. We kids piled out as fast as we could. Grandma met us at the screen door on the porch of their little log house. Grandpa sat in his chair by the window in the kitchen smoking a cigar. He wore blue jean overalls and a train engineer style hat. As soon as he saw Ruthie his face lit up.

"Dink!" He pulled Ruthie into his arms and set her in his lap. Dink was the nickname Grandpa gave her. She beamed and he rubbed his chin whiskers on top of her head as she giggled. Grandpa stood tall and thin and always let his whiskers get pokey. He shaved once a week using a straight razor. The razor strap used for sharpening it hung on the wall above the door in the kitchen. At times he threatened to whoop us with it if we didn't behave but he never took it off the wall except to sharpen his razor. His ears were real big and he always said, "they're stretched that way cause Ma keeps pullin' 'em!"

They didn't have running water and didn't have an indoor bathroom either. They used an outhouse around back at the end of a well worn path. Their water came from a well that they kept covered up with a big piece of plywood. Whenever they needed fresh water we'd follow Grandpa out to the well. He'd pull off the plywood cover and dangle the bucket down into the hole by a rope. It seemed so far down to the water. Grandma always warned us to be careful. Deep down, I think she feared we'd fall in and never get back out again.

Grandma looked like Mom. She kept her light grey hair with a permanent in it. She always wore an apron and support leggings because of her varicose veins. Once I noticed her big toe and the nail on it was split right down the middle. She said it had been that way for years ever since she whacked her toe with an ax once when she chopped some fire wood for the stove.

I stood admiring my Grandma's tiny imitation Christmas tree with its tiny ornaments displayed on top of the buffet table in their small kitchen. The silver tree sparkled with golden ornaments and on top of the tree a miniature silver, star shined, too.

"Come 'ere and take a look see ..." Grandpa said to me as he fumbled with his wallet with Ruthie still sitting on his lap. He pulled out a worn out picture of me. In the photo, my nose glowed red and my eyes were swollen because apparently I didn't want to have my picture taken that day and I'd been crying.

"Who you reckon this is?" He pointed to me in the photo.

"It's me." I smiled at him.

He always showed me the very same picture every time we visited and always asked the very same thing. I guess he thought I might forget myself and that's why he showed me the worn out photo over and over again. He put the picture away and put Ruthie back down on the floor and went back to smoking his cigar. He leaned back in his chair and stared out the kitchen window. I heard him say, "Thank you Lord for this day." I heard him say it almost every time we visited. I don't know for sure if he ever said it when we weren't there or not.

Ruthie and I dashed to the living room to find a spot to sit on the couch. We filled the small house like a can of sardines with all of us inside. A cloud of smoke hung near the ceiling because of the freshly stoked fire in the wood stove. Ruthie and I couldn't find a place to sit in the living room so we snuck into the cold back bedroom that Mom called the Lion's Den. It never got any heat from the wood stove because they kept the bedroom door shut unless there were visitors in the house. An armoire stood in the corner and an antique bed made from beautifully carved wood took up most of the space in the room. Grandma kept her organ in there and sometimes she'd let us play it. An oval mirror hung above an old dresser. Grandma had a large wooden quilt chest in there that she used to store stuff in. We plopped down on the bed and couldn't help but notice the pile of gifts stacked up on the dresser. Ruthie quietly got up and started to fumble through the presents.

"Which is mine?" she asked.

I pretended not to care which one might be mine and started looking for our names on the packages. The names were written in ink pen so I could barely read the writing on some of them. Finally, I found hers. I handed it to her and she sat down with it on the bed turning it every which way trying to figure out what it could be. There didn't seem to be a package with my name on it and my heart began to feel heavy. *Did Grandma forget me?*

Grandma finally went to handing out gifts. Everyone got one except for me. I waited patiently. Grandma smiled and opened up her quilt chest in the Lion's Den. Relief washed over me when I noticed there were more presents in there. She reached inside and pulled out a big present and handed it to me. I didn't have to open it to figure out the contents - a *quilt*. I tore open the paper and there it was - a homemade quilt just for me. Grandma had sewn scrap pieces of material together with a green backing tacked together with blue yarn.

"Thank you Grandma!" I gave her a squeeze.

"It ain't fancy but I hope you like it." She smiled.

"I love it!" I couldn't believe I got a quilt. Grandma made them for her grandchildren when they were getting ready to get married. *Why did I get mine so soon?*

"What did you get?" I asked Ruthie. She held another baby doll up for me to see.

"Awe, she's sweet," I said as she stared at my patchwork quilt.

"She drinks a bottle and pees." She grinned in her ornery way and her brown eyes twinkled.

I couldn't resist, "She better not pee on me!"

"She won't!" She answered and turned around to show her baby off to someone else.

After the presents were opened, we headed home for our Christmas. I suddenly realized that we did have a Christmas tradition. It was our *tradition* to open presents on Christmas Eve at our house.

As we drove back home, all of us were about to bust with excitement wondering what presents were waiting for us at home. I couldn't help but think of my friend, Daniel. What would his Christmas be like without his mother? Plus, I knew there would soon be a funeral and I hated funerals more than just about anything. I felt sorry for Daniel having to see his mother laid out in a casket.

I attended only one funeral in my life and it gave me the creeps. My Great Aunt died of old age. I didn't really know her very well. There were more flowers there than I'd ever seen in my whole life. The smell of all of those flowers made me feel a little sick. Then another smell that I couldn't quite put my finger on lingered there and I didn't like it. Not one little bit.

The grey casket was lined with fluffy silky material that I'd hate to lay on for eternity. I couldn't help noticing that there were locks on the side of the casket that clicked when they closed it shut. I guess they wanted to make sure the dead person didn't get out again.

I wondered, *why did God make us to die?*

It would be a terrible Christmas for Daniel, I just knew it. Then another terrible thought came to me. *What if Mom made us go to the funeral?*

Chapter Twelve
Our Family Christmas

When we got home everyone sat in the living room except Mom. She joyfully went into her bedroom and came back with an armful of wrapped presents. She handed them out one by one and we began tearing into them. I noticed Dad heading back to their bedroom. We were lost in the madness that was *our Christmas* with wrapping paper flying every which way when I remembered my hopes about the piano that I overheard in my parents' bedroom. Maybe Dad planned on wheeling it out at any moment. Mom handed me another present to open. Inside the package I found a pair of double knit pants with a matching shirt.

I looked up again and saw Dad. He was carrying a… *banjo*. He handed it to my older brother and they sat down together and began to fiddle around with it.

It was a banjo.

As the realization hit me, my heart sank to the floor. It wasn't a piano and it wasn't even for me.

Ping, ping, ping. They plunked the strings. My brother's face lit up and Dad couldn't stop smiling as they sat there together playing around with that banjo. I decided that I hated the banjo.

After the craziness of opening presents, I hauled my stash to my bedroom. I received a new outfit, a watch and a Garfield bank. Ruthie came in and showed me her presents.

"What's wrong?" she asked with concern.

"Nothin', I guess." I shrugged my shoulders. She didn't know I expected a piano.

"Lookie at my doll," she held the new doll she got at Grandma's house and took off the wet diaper. "She peed!"

"Cool." I couldn't muster up any excitement.

Then I remembered my new quilt and unfolded it to give it a good look. There, sewn together with many other scraps of material were pieces of my dress Grandma made me for my birthday. I touched the fabric and smiled. It struck me that Grandma put a lot of work into that quilt and I began to treasure it right then and there. Ruthie stared at the quilt.

"Why didn't I get a quilt?" she asked me as she felt of the blue yarn tacking it together.

"I dunno," I answered and really *didn't even know why I got one.*

"Well, I might stop suckin' my thumb if she makes me one," she suggested.

I remembered the training bra in my drawer that Anna Lee gave me in school. The material felt scratchy on my skin after I wore it all day. A thought crossed my mind.

"Would you stop for *this*?" I whipped the training bra out of my drawer and Ruthie's eyes grew as big as saucers.

"Where did you get *that*?!" she scrunched up her nose as if she wasn't interested. Then she took it from my hand and pulled off her shirt. She slid the bra on and I helped her snap it in the back.

"It fits!" She smiled, "Can I have it?"

"If you stop suckin' your thumb…" I told her.

She proudly pranced around the bedroom with the training bra on. I knew exactly how she felt. Like a grown-up. I decided that I wasn't ready to grow up yet. Bras aren't that comfortable.

One of the presents Mom handed me, I decided not to open. I hid it underneath my new outfit. Ruthie caught a glimpse of the wrapping paper as she put her shirt back on over the bra.

"You forgot to open this one." She pulled it out.

"No I didn't." I put it on the dresser by my glittery paper angel and the Polaroid snapshot that Nella gave me.

"Open it!" She stared at me.

"Nah, I'm saving it for Christmas morning. I'm going to open it as soon as I wake up, like normal people do." I sighed.

"Why?" she said dryly. "Can I open it?"

"No, you can't open it." Good night nurse! Couldn't I have Christmas the way I wanted to for crying out loud?

"Humph!" She sat with her thumb stuck back in her mouth then suddenly realized that if she wanted to keep the bra, she couldn't suck her thumb anymore and pulled it back out of her mouth again.

She left the bedroom and came back with part of a roll of wrapping paper and some tape. Then she took her doll and started wrapping it back up.

"What are *you doing*?" I asked, annoyed with her.

"I'm savin' this for tomorrow. I'm gonna open mine when you do." She continued wrapping the present as good as she could. She placed it on the dresser next to mine. "There." She smiled.

"Fine." I left the bedroom and went into the living room. The madness calmed down and the evening news came on the television. I sat in the living room floor and listened. I heard the weather man say that Santa's sleigh showed up on radar and he was headed our way.

What? I couldn't believe it! I'd never heard that on the news before. He pointed to a red spot on the radar screen as it moved across the sky. I looked around the room to see if anyone else heard it or just me. Mom busied herself picking up torn up wrapping paper and Dad still plunked the banjo. Nobody heard it but me. *Santa is coming?* A new hope began to grow inside me as I considered it possible that there might really be a Santa Claus and he might be headed our way.

"Okay - it's time to go to bed! Hit the sack! Pronto!" Mom meant business when she said *Pronto*. I got up and brushed my teeth and crawled into bed next to Ruthie underneath my new quilt. I enveloped myself in its wonderful cool comfort.

All night I kept thinking I heard *sleigh bells*. A couple of times I got up and stared into the night sky looking for a red dot followed by the rest of the reindeer and Santa in his sleigh.

Ruthie tossed and turned and tried hard not to suck her thumb. She slept in the training bra as a reminder. After awhile I heard her snoozing and I didn't hear any smacking. I checked and sure enough, she fell asleep without sucking her thumb. I couldn't believe it. After all the stuff she talked my parents out of to get her to stop, all it took was a hand-me-down training bra.

Finally, I fell asleep too. I dreamed of Grandparents, miniature trees with tiny decorations, banjos, training bras, baby Jesus and paper angels. There wasn't any smacking and so I slept really well and felt loved wrapped up in the patchwork quilt Grandma made me.

When I woke up the first thing I noticed was my unopened present that I saved for Christmas morning next to Ruthie's re-wrapped present. I couldn't wait to open it.

"Ruthie!" I pulled the blanket off of her. "Wake up!"

"I don't have to. Leave me alone." She whined and pulled the blanket.

"It's Christmas!" I reminded her. I wanted to tell her about what the weather man said on the news about Santa heading our way but decided against it. She didn't really know anything much about Santa and, in case it wasn't true, I didn't want to get her hopes up for nothing.

She sat straight up in bed. Her big brown eyes filled with joy. She reached up and grabbed her present that she'd already opened once and tore it open again. "A doll!" She gasped in surprise as if she didn't ever open it before.

"Wow...she's nice," I said and pretended surprise.

I held my unopened present in my hands and began to tear the paper on it very slowly. I wanted Christmas to last a little bit longer. Finally, I could see inside. A beautiful fashion doll stared back at me. Not the kind you play with but the kind you put up on a shelf or on a dresser just to look at. I couldn't stop staring at her. Her hair hung in long blond curls and she wore a pink and white dress with a matching hat. She held a parasol opened up behind her back. How lovely!

"Woe...she's pretty!" Ruthie admired the doll so I let her hold her but just for a minute.

Inside of me, a bubble of hope bounced around. I thought maybe I'd find a stack of presents in the living room. Maybe the weatherman really saw Santa on radar. Maybe Santa came.

We went to the living room to warm up by the wood stove. I carried my doll and Ruthie carried hers. I didn't see any more presents. Santa didn't come. My Christmas bubble of hope *popped.* Just like that. After that, I didn't trust the news people anymore. Especially - the weather man. For a moment, I understood Dad's conviction about all the fuss with Christmas and wondered if maybe he might be right. Maybe. Mom rocked in the recliner and smiled when she saw that I opened my last present. I smiled back. My disappointments about not having a Christmas tree or decorations diminished when I saw all that I did have. My brother plunked on his banjo and Dad and my other brother strummed the guitar. My glamour queen sister sat polishing her nails and my little brother rolled around a new truck on the living room floor. Ruthie and I sat near the stove and admired our new dolls.

I thought about Nella. Surely she'd be calling me later to tell me about all the stuff she got for Christmas and how Santa wrapped hers all in the same kind of wrapping paper. I sorta looked forward to hearing about it because then I could imagine that it was real and that Santa really did come.

"Oh!" My dad put down the guitar and stood up.

"I just remembered somethin'. I heard a racket out back last night and guess who I saw out behind the house messin' around with the well house door?" He smiled.

Ruthie and I both dropped our dolls to the floor. Our eyes and mouths open wide. Could it be?

"Well, I peeked in there and you'll never believe what that ole' feller left in the well house!" He started walking back towards the patio door that led into the back yard. We followed him in disbelief. Cautiously, in case Dad was pulling our leg.

He opened the patio door and then opened the door to the well house. Inside I could see the pink and white basket on the handle bars of a new bike. I gasped and covered my mouth. Ruthie began to squeal and jump up and down. He carried mine in first and brought it inside the house through the back door making sure not to track in any snow. Then he brought Ruthie's inside and hers looked just like mine except for the size and there were miniature training wheels on it.

"I can't believe I got a brand new bike!" I happily climbed onto it. Ruthie climbed on hers, too. Our family gathered around and Mom snapped a picture. Dad stood smiling from ear to ear as Ruthie peddled her bike around the kitchen. After a while Mom busted up the party.

"You'll have to take those outside on the carport so that I can get the turkey in the oven." She motioned for us to get out of the kitchen. Dad carried them outside for us and we stared at them out the living room picture window. There they were sitting on the carport waiting for us to come outside. We'd have to wait until the snow thawed because of our icy driveway. But just staring at them seemed to be enough for us that glorious Christmas morning.

Christmas finally came.

No beautiful decorated tree stood in front of our living room window. No lights hung on my gutters or doorframes but inside I felt all *Christmasee*. No Santa Claus came except for the one that Dad saw and I didn't know for sure if he was telling us the truth or playing along for Ruthie's sake. Plus, I realized that he never said Santa Claus but just that "ole' feller". But either way it didn't matter because we were a happy family.

I thought about Jesus and my new relationship with Him. Then I remembered that I needed to tell Dad about it. I poked him on the shoulder and he put down the guitar again.

"What is it?" He asked.

"I gotta tell you something," I whispered.

"Go ahead."

"Last week, at the Christmas program at my school, I felt the Holy Spirit calling me and I decided to follow Jesus. Not the baby Jesus in the manger, but the grown up Jesus who died for my sins," I shared.

He grabbed me and squeezed me tight, "That's the best Christmas present I could have gotten!" He kissed my cheek. He said we'd talk more about it later and pray together and we'd share it with the church then I'd need to get baptized. I couldn't wait!

Christmas day went by and we feasted on turkey, mashed potatoes and gravy, green beans, buttered rolls and three different kinds of pies. We went to my other Grandparents house and ate dinner there with all of our cousins. Then the big day we'd been waiting so long for ended. I lay down to go to sleep that night and Ruthie didn't suck her thumb and she still wore her training bra.

I thought about all of my longing for decorations and trees.

Christmas came without them.

Not the Christmas I dreamed of with a big tree and decorations and Santa Claus but a good Christmas. *Our Christmas.*

Best of all, I was now one of God's children and I could talk to Him any time I wanted. I really liked knowing that any time a problem caused me grief I could get down on my knees and talk to God about it and know that He would take care of me no matter what. I figured sometimes He might say no and I'd have to work on listening to Him as well as praying to Him. I tried real hard not to sin but it could already see it would be difficult. I was sure I'd be asking Him to forgive me again.

I remembered Daniel and my heart ached for him.

Chapter Thirteen

A Funeral

The day after Christmas was the dreaded day of the funeral for Daniel's mom. Dad said we should all go. I hated funerals and funeral homes and caskets. Nevertheless, I had no choice in the matter and we were going so I got dressed in my best clothes reserved for church on Sundays.

Ruthie asked me to fix her hair. I pulled her blond hair back into pigtails and tied a blue ribbon around each of them that matched her dress. Then I saw my own reflection and wished my glamour queen sister could take the time to fix me up for the funeral. But she busied herself getting ready so I tried to make myself look presentable by pulling my hair into a pony tail. I tied a ribbon around mine, too. I knew the appropriate color to wear to a funeral but I didn't have a black dress. As I dug through my closet I pulled out the closest color to black that I could find. I held up the navy blue plaid skirt with a matching shirt and ruffles hid the buttons down the front. It would have to do and I looked pretty good when I evaluated myself in the mirror.

Once we all piled into the wagon and drove into town, this terrible feeling started coming over me. *Dead people, caskets and funeral homes…I don't want to go!* Dad continued to drive as if he couldn't read my thoughts and before I knew it we were pulling up and parking in the funeral home parking lot on Main Street. The funeral home kept a sign hanging out front with the dead person's name spelled out on it so that anyone driving by would know who died. I read Daniel's mom's name on the sign as we walked toward the front door. Hilda. I never knew her name before that moment. Suddenly, I felt bad for never knowing her name. Now I couldn't even tell her that I was sorry for never knowing her name.

The aroma of fresh flower arrangements hit me as soon as we stepped inside. Dad signed our names in the attendance book with a fancy feather pen as we all stood there waiting for him to finish. My brothers seemed to recognize the solemn occasion and stood as still as I'd ever seen them. Ruthie seemed carefree holding one of her baby dolls wrapped up in a blanket. Mom held my littlest brother in her arms and hushed him with a lollipop. My stomach turned and I felt a powerful urge to rush out the door and never go back into that terrible funeral parlor again. *Why did I feel that way?*

We followed Dad and Mom into the room with the casket and I could see Daniel's family standing up front by his mom's lifeless body. Dad said that I should go up with him to give them my condolences. He held my hand and walked me up to the casket nestled in between two flower lined walls with family standing around. I noticed Daniel's dad. His eyes were red rimmed and he held a handkerchief in his hand which he used every so often to wipe a tear or to wipe his nose. Daniel's eyes weren't red rimmed but he seemed very solemn and more quiet than usual. I shook his hand awkwardly and then hugged his neck. I whispered, "I'm sorry for your loss, Daniel."

He looked at me and said thank you as he nodded his head

thoughtfully then pushed his glasses back up with his finger like he always did in class.

Then Dad went to look at Hilda and took me with him. We stood in front of the casket and took a look at Daniel's mom lying there in state. I couldn't help but notice that she looked hollow somehow. I looked at her makeup covered face and noticed her eyelids seemed forced shut. Her grey streaked hair was pulled back into a bun the way I'd always seen her wear it. She wore a nice blue dress with little yellow flowers on it that buttoned up the front and her hands were closed together across her chest. I noticed the golden wedding ring still on her left finger.

The casket looked just like the one my aunt used at her funeral. The lining looked like the same satiny material that I thought was a terrible choice for lining a casket. Why not use flannel or something soft? Cotton, maybe? The more I thought about it the more I figured that faded blue jean material would be a good casket liner. Nothing could compare to the comfort of a favorite pair of old worn out blue jeans. I decided that was what I wanted to lay on for eternity.

Daniel's little sister sat in the front row with swollen eyes and a runny nose. Her blond hair was almost white and she looked very plain. Her eyelashes were invisible because they were the same color as her hair and the blue eyes behind them seemed even sharper. My heart ached when I saw how downcast she seemed at having to see her mother in a casket. How could she ever be happy again? She sniffed and cried softly as her oldest brother went to her and put his arm around her to comfort her.

"Everything is gonna be okay, Emma. Stop crying. I'm here with you," he said softly as he gently rubbed her back. James, the oldest of the three children, was the happy child in the family. He played the piano brilliantly for his age and made good grades, too. The two younger ones seemed to have a harder time getting along in the world.

More people were coming up to pay their respects so Dad took me back to sit down with the family in the last row of chairs. I sat down by Ruthie and stared up at the scene in front of me. There were flowers, flowers and more flowers. Every kind of flower I knew of seemed to be lining the wall on both sides of the casket. There were plants with nice cards written out to the family and even a few stuffed animals along the wall. I guess some folks thought the kids might get comfort from them. A group of older women behind me began to have a conversation and I overheard their hushed whispers.

"It was a terrible thing. Leaving them three young children without a mother," one tall woman said with her mouth half covered to the other three women who listened intently.

"I know, I know.....it's a crying shame. That's what it is," a shorter woman with black hair piled up on top of her head said to the group. Her nose was too long for her face and her nostrils flared as she spoke. Then I heard something that shocked me.

"You know there's nothing on this earth worth facing the fires of hell over but that's what Hilda's doing right now. Bless her soul!" Her high pitched whisper made my eyes grow wide in horror.

"Now, Betty, you don't know that. You shouldn't say things like that especially in the presence of the dead." A blond older woman stepped up to defend the helpless dead woman. "That's a matter of opinion."

"Well, if she didn't ask for forgiveness then I'm sorry to say it but she's burning in hell," Betty said, certain that she knew all the ramifications of not asking for forgiveness for every sin one commits.

A quiet argument broke out and I couldn't believe my ears. Dad listened too because he glanced at my horror stricken face and gently shook his head as if to say, "No, no, no." It comforted me for a moment but I couldn't help but listen to the rest of the conversation.

"You have to ask for forgiveness for your sins or else you're going to hell." Betty stated again. "That's religion – 101."

Then the older blond woman seemed to lose her patience, "Betty, do you mean to tell me that every time you sin you ask God for forgiveness at that very moment? I don't think so! There are many sins you commit against God that you are completely *unaware* of. If what you're saying is true then nobody has a chance in hell of making it to heaven!" She huffed and Betty shrunk at the other woman's harsh words toward her.

"Well, I never!" Betty gasped and removed herself from the group. She took a seat across the room. The women who were left began to chastise her behind her back.

"I never heard of anything so darn *dumb* in my life." The blond woman whispered loudly as she looked for acknowledgement from the group.

"Yes, it's true. There's no way that we can always be aware of our sinful natures enough to ask for forgiveness for everything. I'd hate to think that I unknowingly sinned against God and drove off down the road, got killed and found myself in the fiery furnaces of hell because I didn't even realize what I'd done in the first place." She rolled her eyes and then went on thoughtfully and seemed full of the spirit as she said, "God has *saved us by His grace* and His mercy is more than we deserv

Praise God for that. Praise God that He forgives us for past, present and future sins or else we'd all be doomed to hell."

"Amen, sister." The women all agreed and I suddenly felt glad again.

They made their way up front to where the dead woman lay to give their condolences to Daniel's family. Dad reached over and patted me on the shoulder. He didn't need to say anything. Once, he told me that when we become Christians, our sins are as far away from us as the East is from the West.

The service began and I discovered that Hilda was a Christian, like me. She surrendered her life to Him a long time ago and her sins were forgiven too. It gave me peace to know that at that very moment, she was with Jesus and not burning in those terrible fires of hell for being sad and not asking forgiveness for it.

When the preacher finished everyone walked out single file by the casket to say a final goodbye to Daniel's mom, Hilda. As I stood to walk out in line with my family, my heart was heavy for Daniel and his brother and sister. They stood up and were suddenly taken with the overwhelming grief of never seeing their beloved mother again. Each of them held tissues to their eyes and the tears poured out. I looked at Daniel's mom as I passed by. Then I hoped I never saw another dead person as long as I lived. I hated funerals. I hated funeral homes. I hated caskets and I hated death. If I could avoid the whole thing in the future then I'd figure out a way to do it.

Dad drove us home and Ruthie got sleepy and the baby cried for some food. Mom said we needed to get home and skip the burial. I was glad. I didn't want to go to the graveyard and see them lower the casket into the ground and cover it up with dirt. The whole thing got me to thinking about my sister who died as a baby and how much it must have hurt Mom and Dad.

Before I went to sleep that night, I knelt down to pray to God. My mind overflowed with thoughts of death and hell.

Dear God,
Thank you for saving me.
In Jesus name,
Amen.

It was all I really wanted to say. I crawled into bed beneath my new quil with Ruthie snoozing and I closed my eyes and willed myself to dream something peaceful and beautiful. No more thoughts of funerals, death or hell.

Chapter Fourteen
A baby is born

The phone rang again in the middle of the night. *Weasel!* Only this time he wasn't mad - he was happy.

"Kate's at the hospital having the baby!" I heard Mom say and then my parents left us at home with my glamour sister to baby sit us while they went to see their first grandchild.

"Everybody get on back to bed," my parents advised us as they left the house. "We'll call as soon as she has it." They pulled out of the driveway and I listened until I couldn't hear the car engine any longer. A baby was being born. I couldn't wait to see it!

I tried to sleep but couldn't stop thinking of my sister and *Weasel*. I wondered what kind of dad he'd be. I knew my sister would be a great mom but *Weasel*? It took some imagining on my part to see him as a dad. All I saw was a jerk. I guess I just saw his bad side. Something made my sister fall in love with him.

When I woke up my parents were back home sitting at the table drinking coffee and eating some doughnuts they'd picked up in town at Dad's favorite doughnut shop.

"Good morning, Aunt Anna!" Mom announced as I made my way into the kitchen yawning. "It's a girl!"

"Awe! Is she cute? What's her name? Is she okay?" I asked

excitedly as Mom pulled me into her lap. I couldn't remember the last time she did that. I'd grown a lot and there were two younger kids always vying for her lap so she surprised me when she sat me there. It felt nice and comforting. She held me close and squeezed me.

"Her name is Hope. She's perfect. And you know what? So are you," she said and then whispered in my ear, "I love you."

"I love you, too," I responded softly. I really needed to hear that she loved me for some reason.

A few days later, *Weasel* and Kate brought the baby to the house for us to see. We all sat around the living room taking turns holding the baby. She was so beautiful that I couldn't believe it. She seemed very tiny to me and *fragile*. When my turn came to hold her I held her in my arms with great care. I didn't want to drop her on her head or something worse.

"Hold her head like this." My sister showed me how to hold her wobbly little head. I held the baby while I sat perfectly still. She yawned and I laughed. I inhaled her sweet baby breath and it seemed like something straight from heaven. My sister sat down next to me and *Weasel* sat across the room by Dad. He watched me holding the baby and I wondered what he thought about being a dad. The look on his face revealed new found pride of his baby girl and his wife.

Finally I gave the baby back to my sister and then Ruthie took a turn at holding her. Kate held the baby's head for Ruthie for support and so she didn't accidentally move it the wrong way. Ruthie gleamed with pride as she held a baby for the first time. After holding all of those baby dolls she'd gotten for Christmas she actually got to hold the real thing in her arms. When she finished holding her, she couldn't stop smiling. Sh marched straight to our bedroom and brought back one of her baby dolls wrapped in a blanket and held her, pretending that she had a real baby to take care of.

Weasel gently rubbed my sister's back when he sat next to her on the couch. He showed a side of himself that I'd never seen before. I sighed. They seemed to be a happy family. I hoped that it would last.

Chapter Fifteen

An awakening

It seemed to be a new beginning. New Year's Eve celebrations were taking place and our family planned to stay up late, eat homemade popcorn, and watching the ball drop in New York City on television. I never got to stay up till midnight. Ruthie tried but I could see that she'd never make it. She sat on the couch with her hand full of popcorn, her head tilted to the side and popcorn slowly dropped out of her hand as she nodded off. Dad finally picked her up and carried her to our bedroom and tucked her into bed.

I knew for sure that she'd pee the bed because she didn't get a chance to go to the bathroom before she fell asleep.

I didn't let it dampen my spirits though. I was still wide eyed and bushy tailed ready to make it to the New Year! I fell asleep sometime after that. Mom woke me up right before the ball dropped so that I wouldn't miss it. The countdown started and everyone counted. Ten, nine, eight, seven, six, five, four, three, two, one…HAPPY NEW YEAR!!!

We jumped up and down with excitement until finally Mom said, "Okay! Now everyone get to bed!" I yawned and gladly crawled into the nice warm bed where Ruthie snoozed already. She still wore the training bra and I guessed she'd never take it off because she didn't want it to g lost in the laundry room.

The next morning everyone slept in longer than usual and we awoke to a wonderful miracle. *Weasel* knocked on our front door with Kate and the new baby. When I saw them standing there I couldn't imagine what they were doing at our house on New Year's Day. Weasel held a look on his face of pure joy. I couldn't imagine what made him so bright and happy this early in the morning. Dad invited them in and Weasel couldn't contain his excitement any longer.

"He's awake!" He announced and Kate smiled as she sat down next to him on the couch. The baby slept in a baby carrier on the floor covered up with a pink, fuzzy blanket.

"Who? *Who* is awake?" Dad asked curiously.

Mom joined us from the kitchen to hear the astonishing news.

"Jonathan! He's awake!" Weasel and Kate were so happy and full of joy that I couldn't believe it. *Who in the world is Jonathan*, I wondered.

Mom's jaw dropped open.

"He came out of the coma?" Mom asked and Dad slapped his knee with glee at the thought.

"Yes!" *Weasel* excitedly began to tell us how his brother, Jonathan, woke up in the middle of the night and asked the nurse for a drink of water. He said that his mouth was dry.

The vegetable! I thought. He woke up! Relief flooded through me when I realized that he was awake! Those horrible thoughts of him not being able to wake up were never to be thought of again because he was awake and he could speak! His brain *must* be better if he could speak.

"Dad and Mom are with him right now and we're on our way in

town to go see him." Weasel said, busting with excitement. I'd never seen him like that ever in my entire life. The pressure seemed to be off of him for driving the car that night. I figured he must have asked God to forgive him. Then I wondered if maybe he finally forgave himself.

"Let's all go see him!" Dad announced. My eyebrows raised in astonishment because I'd never even met Jonathan but I guessed it would be nice to meet him now that he wasn't a vegetable anymore. I ran to my room to get dressed and Ruthie did too.

Before I knew it we were all getting out of the car at the nursing home where Jonathan was because of his coma. I hated hospitals and nursing homes, too. But I swallowed my fear and looked ahead as we walked down the long hall toward Jonathan's room. I heard lots of folks talking about Jonathan and his miraculous waking up. *Weasel* and Kate were holding their heads high as they walked into his room and *Weasel'* parents gave them both a hug. The joy of it all beamed all over both of their faces. Then I saw Jonathan lying there in the hospital bed. He looked very thin with his eyes slightly open. A grin spread across his face when he saw Weasel and Kate.

Weasel went to Jonathan and hugged his neck. He began to weep and tears were pouring down *Weasel's* cheeks. Jonathan was still hooked up to some machines and I wasn't sure what they all did either. watched for awhile and when *Weasel* withdrew from his brother there were tears on Jonathan's cheeks, too. *Brotherly love*, I thought. My hea ached but it with a happy ache and not like the kind I felt at the funeral for Daniel's mom.

The crowded room overflowed into the hallway. I couldn't help peeking in and listening to the grownup conversation about the awakening. That's when I heard Jonathan speak.

"Bay…" He began to form the word and then tried again as a smile crept across his face. "Ba…by…" He finished as he raised his arm slowly and pointed to Hope in her pumpkin seat carrier. Weasel and Kate smiled and gave him a closer look at their new bundle of joy.

"This is a miracle from God. It's a miracle! Jonathan knows us! He remembers things that I hardly even remember!" Jonathan's dad remarked. A wide smile spread across his face and his bright, white false teeth shined.

"It was all the prayers that woke him up," Jonathan's mom concluded as she patted her son's limp hand. He slowly curled his hand around hers the best way that he could and a tear spilled down her cheek.

Prayers?

Suddenly, I remembered that *I prayed* for Jonathan to wake up. I'd asked God to wake him up so that he wouldn't be a vegetable anymore. I was stunned as the realization hit me. God answered my prayer. He answered *my prayer*! Now I became elated at the thought. God really does answer prayers! He listened to me and answered my prayer! I wanted to tell someone about it but realized that I didn't tell anyone at the time. Nobody knew about the heartfelt prayer except me and God. No one would believe that *my prayer* did the trick but I knew it was true!

A joy began to rise up in me that I'd never felt before in my life. Right there among my family standing in the hallway of the nursing home I began to dance. It started with a little shake of my hips as I allowed myself to be overtaken by the rising joy inside me. I jumped up and down and stepped down the hall in a rhythmic fashion as my siblings stared and began to laugh. Then I turned around and faced them and did my very best *Funky Chicken* dance. My hands were tucked up inside my armpits and I flapped them up and down while I moved my legs in and out.

I saw an old man in the room across the hall sitting up in his bed, staring at me with a big smile on his face and not a tooth inside of his mouth. He nodded me on and began to clap his hands.

Then I joined my brothers and sisters as they laughed at me but Mom broke up the party. She stuck her head outside the door and stared at me in disbelief.

"Stop that right now! This is a nursing home and we're supposed to be quiet..." She hushed me by placing her finger on her lips after she scolded me for my outrageous behavior.

Ruthie dropped her doll by this time and danced with me. I looked at her happy brown eyes gleaming. She got caught up in the dance but with no idea what made me so happy. She didn't care. After the scolding, she picked her doll back up, wrapped the blanket back around it and held it to her chest using her best Mom imitation. I smiled. I was glad she stepped out and followed me in my happy dance!

"What was that about?" My glamour queen sister laughed.

I thought about it for a second and then answered, "Nothing!" I wasn't ready to explain my joy just yet. It seemed like such a special thing that God answered my personal prayer that I wasn't sure if I should share it or keep it to myself and savor it. For the moment, I wanted to savor it. The God who created the universe listened to my prayer and decided to wake up the vegetable! I couldn't ask for more than that!

We left the nursing home and I still couldn't believe what happened. I listened intently to Mom and Dad's conversation as we drove home.

"They said after some physical therapy he should be almost back to normal. It's a miracle." Dad seemed astonished as he spoke.

"I can't believe it. The last I heard there was no way he could come out of it. Too much damage and the chance of recovery was practically zero," Mom declared.

Dad cleared his throat, "Well, that's the power of prayer."

Yes! I thought. Dad understood. I was glad to be a Christian and to know God.

Chapter Sixteen

A New Beginning

I laid in bed that night thinking about God. I was drawn to my knees to thank Him for answering my prayer.

Dear God,

Thank you for answering my prayer and waking up the vegetable! I can hardly believe it's true but it is! You've made Weasel and Kate very happy and everyone else it seems. I guess we don't get to see many miracles these days but You did it. You can do anything!

My heart sure is full of joy. That's all I wanted to say. Thank you!

In Jesus' name,

Amen.

Ruthie snoozed and so I soon drifted off into peaceful slumber. I dreamed that I could fly and flew all over the world to foreign places. Anytime I slowed down too much, I'd start flapping my arms as fast as could until I got the momentum back that I needed to continue flying around the world. I never wanted to wake up.

The next morning Nella knocked at my door as I sat eating breakfast. She let herself in as usual and stood next to me while I finished eating.

"Hurry," she urged me.

"I'm eating as fast as I can," I answered and rolled my eyes.

"Let's go to your room and talk."

"I'm done," I said and slurped down the milk in my bowl of cereal.

I went to my room and she followed me, right on my heels the whole way. She closed the door behind us. Ruthie was in the living room watching cartoons so she didn't realize we were sneaking to the bedroom to talk.

"Tell me about Weasel's brother," she instructed as soon as she closed the door. "I heard he woke up and you all went to see him."

"He did wake up." I didn't know how she'd heard already. "I can't believe it." My sweater made my hair full of static as I pulled it on over the top of my head. She busted out laughing and I did too when I felt my hair sticking out everywhere. I pulled on jeans and put socks on while she put her hands on the sides of my hair and tried to get the hair to stop flying up. I grabbed a rubber band and pulled my hair into a ponytail to hold it in place. Then we sat down on the bed and talked.

"What did he look like? Was he all decrepit?" She scrunched up her nose in disgust.

"Well, he looked pretty good, I thought. He was very thin though and he seemed to be very weak. He didn't move much but he did speak." I filled her in on the details as best as I could. Suddenly, I wanted to share with her about my prayer but I wasn't sure how she'd react. We'd argued many times about religion and the Bible. Partly because I was Primitive Baptist and she was Missionary Baptist but mostly because we liked to argue.

"If I tell you something will you promise not to laugh?" I asked as sincerely as I could.

"Humph! Of course, I won't laugh. What is it?" she inquired.

"Well, since I became a Christian, I've been praying a lot about different things. Mostly about Christmas trees but I also prayed for other things. It seemed that God wasn't listening to me. But I kept on praying and talking to him wondering when He would answer me......*if* He would answer me." I stopped and looked into her eyes to see if I could read what her reaction would be. I couldn't. She stared at me and hung on my words. She nodded at me to continue.

"I prayed that the vegetable would wake up after Mom told me that he was in a coma and *couldn't wake up*. Not even to go to the bathroom. I hated that and wanted God to fix it. So, I asked Him one night in my prayers to please wake up the vegetable." I swallowed.

"Then while we were at the nursing home after he was awake, I remembered the prayer when Jonathan's mom said that it was the prayers that woke him up. I knew that it was my prayer that did the trick!"

Nella stared at me in astonishment. She shook her head in disbelief but yet she said, "Wow! That's so awesome. God answered your prayer!"

Relief flooded through me as I realized that she believed me. There wasn't going to be an argument about any facts. She just believed me.

We decided to go for a walk and we were best friends that day. I told her my secret and I believed she'd keep it. It seemed like a new beginning of a better friendship. Maybe we were both growing up a little.

When school started back up a week later I could still fill the joy over the awakening. I went to my classroom and wanted to share it with everyone but since Shirley is a small place, everyone already heard about it.

The Christmas tree no longer stood in our classroom and a disappointment settled inside of me. After the bell rang, Mrs. Wise welcomed us all back to class after Christmas break.

"Did everyone have a good Christmas?" she asked with a smile.

"Yes!" we all answered in unison.

I noticed that Daniel seemed to be his normal quiet self. He wasn't crying or anything like I thought I would be if my mom died. *Maybe he's cried enough already*, I thought. He wore a glow in the dark watch and told me that Santa Claus left it for him. When the school bus went by his house that morning, I noticed that all of their Christmas decorations were still up. I figured they were trying to stay cheerful under the circumstances of the death and all.

"Good!" Mrs. Wise said, "I did too. But it's a new year and we've got lots of work to do!" she announced and we all groaned.

"Now please get your reading books out and turn to page 125. We'll begin with Anna Lee reading the first two paragraphs." Mrs. Wise looked toward Anna Lee who smiled and began to read.

I drifted as she read and thought about how God answered my prayer. A light bulb went off in my head as I considered how powerful prayer was. Maybe if I started praying now then God might overturn Dad's conviction about Christmas trees by *next* Christmas!

A smile spread across my face at the thought.

Made in the USA
Charleston, SC
22 November 2013